PRAISE FOR SING SOMETHING TRUE

"A sunny, heartfelt celebration of the joys and sorrows of friendship, sisterhood and self-discovery."

– Laura Ruby, two-time National Book Award Finalist

"A tender, heartfelt ballad about sisterhood, friendship and authenticity, *Sing Something True* is that special book you want to read over and over."

– Carolyn Crimi, author of *Weird Little Robots*

"The name says it all: *Sing Something True* melds themes of self-expression and integrity with sweetness and grace. Readers will connect with Cass's struggle to be a good friend, sister, and daughter without forgetting something even more important: to be good to herself."

– Lisa Jenn Bigelow, author of *Hazel's Theory of Evolution* and winner of the Lamda Literary Award

"Few writers sing of family and friendship heartache more truthfully and tenderly than Brenda Ferber does here."

– Claudia Mills, author of *Write This Down*

"*Sing Something True* is a joyous ode to sisterly love, a refreshing riff on Queen Bees and BFFs, and a soaring anthem to the power of being your own best friend. Readers will fall in love with Cassidy Sunshine!"

– Jenny Meyerhoff, author of the Friendship Garden series.

"Like every great song, Ferber's heartfelt *Sing Something True* strikes all the right notes. I cheered for Cassidy as she navigated the challenges of family and friendship and, in the process, found her own true voice, clear and empathetic and strong. Right now, we all need a little Cassidy Sunshine in our lives!"

– Sarah Aronson, author of *The Wish List* series and winner of the Crystal Kite Award

"Brenda Ferber's sweet *Sing Something True* hits all the right notes."

– Kate Hannigan, Golden Kite Award winning author of *The Detective's Assistant*

"Whether you have a disabled child in your life or not, this book will sing something true straight to your heart until the very last page."

– Katie Davis, author, illustrator, podcaster, and Director/CEO of Institute for Writers

"With pitch-perfect middle grade voice, Brenda Ferber's *Sing Something True* is a beautiful, authentic, page-turning story of friendship, family ties and a girl discovering what it means to sing your own song."

– Christina Mandelski, author of *The Sweetest Thing, The First Kiss Hypothesis, Love and Other Secrets,* and *Stuck with You*

SING SOMETHING TRUE

Brenda A. Ferber

Fitzroy Books

Published by Fitzroy Books
An imprint of
Regal House Publishing, LLC
Raleigh, NC 27612
All rights reserved

https://fitzroybooks.com

Printed in the United States of America

ISBN -13 (paperback): 9781646030613
ISBN -13 (epub): 9781646030866
Library of Congress Control Number: 2020940211

Interior and cover design by Lafayette & Greene
lafayetteandgreene.com
Cover images © by C.B. Royal

 Regal House Publishing, LLC
https://regalhousepublishing.com

Printed in the United States of America

For the Four Baers: Micky, Jeff, Riley, and Billie
I love you!
xoxo
(Aunt) Bren

Contents

Chapter One

Last spring, my sister and I made a bird feeder for the tree outside my bedroom window, and after that, a family of robins woke me up each morning with their happy tweeting. Most days, I would lie in bed listening to them sing to each other. Sometimes I would sing along. It always sounded like they were having a conversation, and I wished I knew what they were saying. Maybe they were making plans or talking about the plump worms they'd found or telling each other, *I love you. You're amazing*. For those few minutes each morning, the birds made me feel like things were just right and might even stay that way.

Then one morning it got weird. I heard only one lonely chirp.

I pulled up my blinds to investigate. It was the middle of October, so the leaves were golden yellow. One robin perched on a branch right outside my window. The rest of the birds were nowhere in sight. The robin kept opening his beak and chirping in a way that seemed to say, *Hey! Hey, you! Listen to me!*

Poor bird, all alone. I waved to him and said, "Good morning, robin. Where's your family today?"

The robin fluttered off the branch, spun around, and landed there again. Then he chirped-chirped-chirped, like he was trying to talk to me.

What a funny little bird. And how strange that the others were missing. I peered out, searching in every direction, but the robin was all by himself. He seemed lonely. And mad.

"Don't worry, little bird," I said, as if he could understand me. "You'll find your family. Maybe they went to a different tree this morning. You should go look for them."

The robin cocked his head, then flew away.

It was quiet without his chirping, so I hummed a tune to shake off the lonely feeling he'd given me. I put on my favorite jeans and a hand-me-down top from my sister, Sophie, one with emojis all over it. I hoped today would be a smiley face kind of day and not a poop one. If I got to school before first bell, I'd have a chance for smileys. Otherwise, Dani and Lucy would hang out without me again. Poop emoji for sure.

I had a wobbly feeling in my chest just thinking about those two. I had to make sure my sister had a good morning, so I could be on time for school, and things might be halfway normal with my friends. Specifically, with my best friend, Dani. And with the new girl, the intruder, Lucy London.

I went across the hall to Sophie's room. Mom had already turned on her light, but Sophie was hiding under her blanket on the floor. My big sister almost always ended up sleeping on the floor even though she started each night in her bed. I wasn't sure which part of her disability made that happen, but it was a thing.

I went in and tilted open her blinds. "Soph! Wake up!"
She groaned.

"Come on!" I pulled the blanket off her face and smiled down at her. "Morning!"

She squinted and threw her arm over her eyes. "Too bright."

"It's sunshine. It's good." I pictured the sun warming the blacktop at school. That's where we all gathered before first bell, and on Mondays it was where everyone talked about the fun they had on the weekend. Lucy and Dani would be talking about their sleepover for sure. "Come on, I'll race you to breakfast."

Sophie moved her arm down and opened her eyes. "No fair, Cass. You're already dressed."

"I'll wait for you."

Sophie stretched and stood. I hopped from one foot to the

2

other while she pulled on a black velvet top over silver leggings. Sophie was only a year older than me, but she was a whole head taller. We got most of our clothes from our older cousins, but Sophie managed to put her own flair on things. When we were little, my sister said she felt like the necks of her shirts were choking her, so Mom pretended to be a fashion designer while she cut them out, making wider openings without the annoying seams. Now Sophie thought *she* was a fashion designer. She said clothes were art and that everyone at school knew she was an artist, even if they didn't all appreciate it. Lately she'd been into accessories, so this morning she added a silver sequined scarf from last year's Halloween costume to complete her look.

I said, "You look pretty. Now, on your mark, get set—"

But Sophie was already out her bedroom door and past me, shouting, "Go!"

I didn't care. As long as Sophie was moving and in a good mood, my day had a chance of being great.

ॐ

"Morning, girls!" Mom said. "Waffles or eggs?" She was standing at the kitchen counter, drinking coffee and looking at her computer. Her hair was pulled into a low side ponytail, and she was wearing work clothes—black slacks and a crisp white blouse.

"Eggs," Sophie said. "Over easy, please-y." She laughed.

"Waffles," I said. "I'll make them myself." I opened the freezer, took two cinnamon waffles out of the box, and popped them into the toaster.

Mom raised her eyebrows.

"Mrs. Kwon says fifth graders should be more self-reliant," I told her. I got out a plate and filled a glass with orange juice. Mrs. Kwon would be proud.

"I'm all for that." Mom pulled the frying pan out of the cabinet.

"Wait," Sophie said. "I want to make my own eggs."

"Oh, Soph, not today. Teaching you how to fry eggs is a weekend activity."

"I can do it." Sophie got the eggs out of the refrigerator. "After all, I'm in *sixth* grade." She said it as if sixth grade was eons past fifth. "Now, what do I do first?"

Mom put her hand up. Her nostrils flared the way they did when she was annoyed but trying to be patient. "Sophie, I mean it. We don't have time for a big mess. If you want eggs, I'm making them. If you want waffles, you can make them yourself. The choice is yours."

"But I love eggs!" Sophie's face turned red. Her hands clenched into fists. "Mom! I want to make eggs! I *have* to make eggs!"

My muscles got all tense. A Super Sophie Tantrum was hard any time of day, but mornings were the worst. It made the whole day get off on the wrong foot. Not to mention we'd be late, and Dani and Lucy might plan another sleepover.

I put a napkin, fork, and knife on the table and took the syrup out of the pantry. I kept my eyes away from Sophie. I knew if she saw me paying attention to her, it would only make things worse. I took a deep breath and started to sing "Summer Sky" very softly. That was the song I was working on in my voice lessons. Singing always made me happy, no matter what was going on around me.

Mom said, "Waffles or eggs, Soph? I'm counting to three. One…two…"

Here's what I thought would happen next: Mom would get to three, Sophie would fall to the floor in tears, and a Super Sophie Tantrum would begin.

Here's what actually happened: Sophie said, "Fine! EGGS!"

It was a miracle. The toaster dinged. My muscles relaxed, and it felt like my body was filled with little golden bubbles. I put the waffles on my plate.

Mom handed me a banana.

I twirled my way over to the table and ate my breakfast.

Sophie sat at the table and sulked. Sulking was okay. Sulking was practically nothing. I checked the clock. "We're leaving in fifteen minutes," I said, and Sophie nodded.

Mom put Sophie's breakfast and her medicine on the table. Sophie took medicine for SPD, sensory processing disorder, which made her brain act like a broken thermometer. Little things felt like big things to Sophie, and when her broken thermometer spiked too high, she lost control of her emotions. It was called being dysregulated. I learned that word before I knew how to tie my shoes.

Sophie's tantrums weren't her fault, but I hated them. And sometimes, even though I knew I shouldn't, I hated Sophie for having them. They weren't like a two-year-old's tantrums. For one thing, Sophie was eleven. For another, she was strong. Plus, she never ran out of steam. If tantrums were an Olympic sport, Sophie could win the gold medal. The medicine helped. And so did I. Mom and Dad too. Debra, her therapist. Jackie, her occupational therapist. And Miss Michelle, her aide at school. We all worked hard to help Sophie stay regulated.

Sophie stuck a fork in her egg and the yolk oozed out. "Uh-oh, Mom. It's too runny."

"You said over-easy."

"But it's liquidy."

"That's what over-easy means, Soph. Do you want me to cook them longer?"

"No. I'm not hungry."

Warning bells rang in my head. Sophie could be starving and say she wasn't hungry because of any teeny tiny thing like, say, runny eggs. And a hungry Sophie was soon to be a dysregulated Sophie.

"Do you want one of my waffles?" I asked.

"No thanks."

Mom came over and sat next to Sophie. She used her calm voice. "Sophie, please take your medicine."

Sophie swallowed her pills.

"Thank you. Now, you know you need to eat a good breakfast in order to have a good day at school, right?"

Sophie nodded.

"So how about I cook these eggs a little longer for you?"

Sophie shook her head.

"Okay then, how about a bowl of cereal?"

"I'M! NOT! HUNGRY!" Sophie pushed her plate away, but she used so much force that it flipped over and clattered, and runny eggs spilled onto the table.

My breath caught in my throat.

"Look what you made me do!" Sophie yelled.

"Sophie, shhh!" Mom grabbed paper towels to clean the mess. "It's fine."

"IT'S NOT FINE!"

The waffles turned to rocks in my stomach.

Dad came into the kitchen. He worked from home, and he did video calls with people in India and China, so mornings were his busy time. We were supposed to be quiet because his office was right next to the kitchen.

"I was on an important call," he said to Mom, as if she were the one having the tantrum. Dad was wearing his usual work outfit of a button-down shirt and tie, paired with pajama pants. "I had to hang up by pretending the connection was bad."

"I'm sorry," Mom snapped. "But it's not like I planned this." Her calm voice was nowhere to be found. She turned to Sophie. "Enough already. You need to eat. I don't have time for this today."

"Nooooo! I caaaaan't!" Tears streamed down her face.

My jaw hurt, which made me realize I was clenching my teeth. I cleared my place. I didn't have time for this either. As I rinsed my dish I wondered why everything in our house had to turn into yelling and crying. But I guess I knew. SPD. I wished it had never been invented.

I opened the junk drawer in my mind, the one where I kept all my bad thoughts and feelings, and I shoved this one in with the others. I slammed the drawer shut.

Then I took a big breath and went upstairs.

I always walked to school with Sophie. But maybe today I wouldn't. Maybe today she could walk by herself, and I would get there on time. Then I'd hang with Dani and Lucy and stop them from going on and on about their dumb sleepover. Next year, Sophie and I wouldn't even be going to the same school. She'd have to take a bus to middle school. So sooner or later she'd have to get used to not having me by her side. Why not today?

I brushed my teeth and hair.

Downstairs, Sophie kept crying.

I came back down, packed my backpack, and put on my jean jacket.

Sophie kept screaming.

I skipped kissing Mom and Dad goodbye because I didn't want them to tell me to wait for Sophie. Plus, they were busy trying to keep her from hurting herself or anything else in the kitchen. We already had a dent in the wall and a cabinet that hung lopsided, both from past tantrums.

I opened the front door, and in my most sunshiny voice, I called out, "Bye! I'm leaving. Have a good day."

Just as the door was about to shut behind me, Sophie shouted, "Don't leave without me, Cass! Pleeeeeeaaaase!"

I turned around. Her face was red and wet with tears, her hair a wild mess. Her desperate eyes begged me to wait.

My sister.

This wasn't her fault.

And then, the thought that always bopped me on the nose when I least wanted it: I could be the one with SPD.

I thought about Dani and Lucy. I hated being left out. It made me feel like I was…I don't know, replaceable. But that was stupid. Dani wouldn't replace me. You don't just drop your best friend since kindergarten for the first interesting girl who moves to town. Still, if I kept giving Dani and Lucy chances to hang out without me, there was no telling what might happen.

My heart twisted.

Sophie was still looking at me with hope in her eyes.

Family came first. And Sophie needed me.

"I'll wait for you outside," I said, then closed the door behind me.

Chapter Two

My body felt heavy. I walked to the end of the driveway, far enough away from our house that Sophie's cries couldn't reach me, and I plopped down on the grass. The air was cool and autumny, but the sun was warm. Lots of kids passed our house on their way to school, which was just half a block away. Most of them were already there, playing before first bell, but a few stragglers hurried past. I kept my eyes down and watched an ant carry a breadcrumb twice his size across the sidewalk.

I listened to shouts from the playground. I couldn't make out their voices, but I was sure Dani and Lucy were there, having fun without me. Lucy's mom had let her invite only one person to sleep over. If Lucy London had invited just me, I wouldn't have gone. I'd have asked her to come to my house instead so we could have included Dani. Not that sleepovers at my house ever worked out. But Lucy and I could have *both* slept at Dani's. I didn't know why Dani hadn't suggested that.

Maybe she wanted to see where Lucy lived, what her room was like. I sure did. There was something about Lucy London that made us all want to know her better. I called it the Lucy-factor. Dani called it charisma and said that Lucy had stage presence, which made no sense because we weren't on a stage.

When I got left out of the sleepover, Mom had said, "Sometimes that's how things go, honey."

But I didn't want things to go like that. I wanted to be included. Lucy wouldn't feel like an intruder to me if we were friends, too. I didn't need to have Dani all to myself. We could all three be friends.

Leaves rustled and fell in the breeze. The only people crossing my way were parents or nannies coming back from dropping off their kids. They were busy on their phones, not paying attention to me, so I opened my backpack, took out my voice recorder, and pressed play.

I always recorded my voice lessons so I could play them back while I practiced during the week. My teacher said that's what professional singers do. It was helpful because I got to hear my voice from outside my head instead of inside it, which was a whole different sound. Plus, I could have Javier playing guitar and listen again to all of his hints and reminders. Javier was from Cuba, just like Dani's parents, and he rolled his Rs when he said things like, "Remember to breathe from your diaphragm, my friend."

I listened to him say that while he strummed the opening chords to "Summer Sky" by Ruby Maguire, a folksinger I love.

I put my hand on my belly, to be sure I was breathing right, and sang along. I loved to sing this song, even though my voice didn't sound anything like Ruby's. We both had high and clear voices, but Ruby's was really strong. It had weight behind it. Mine was more like a thread pulled tight.

As I sang, the bad feelings from Sophie's tantrum and Lucy and Dani's sleepover washed away, and I felt lighter.

In the middle of the second verse, a robin circled overhead and landed in front of me. Was it the same robin? He cocked his head to the side and stared at me, like he was listening to me sing, which made me giggle and stop. But my voice on the recorder kept going. The bird hopped closer, eyeing the recorder. I was pretty sure he was the bird I'd seen outside my window earlier. He had a bright orange chest, brown feathers, and white circles around his black eyes. One of the circles had a missing piece at the top.

"You didn't find your family?" I asked him.

The robin looked from the recorder to me, then back again. It was like he was figuring out how my singing voice was coming out of it. He hopped closer still and chirped. I'd never been so near a bird before. His feathers twitched, and his head bobbed.

The bird tapped on my voice recorder with his beak. I grabbed the recorder—I thought he might break it—and pressed stop. He flew up in the air, floated for a second, then landed a few feet away from me. He looked at me and chirped, as if he were saying, *What did you do that for?*

This was one strange bird. He was more like a timid dog or cat than a robin in the wild. But the way he was talking to me, I mean chirping at me…it was like he wanted something.

"What do you want, little bird?" I asked, scooting closer.

He chirped again. I wished I understood.

"Do you need help finding your family?" I plucked a piece of grass and twirled it between my fingers. I didn't know how I'd help him find his family, if that's what he even wanted.

I looked at the bird. He looked at me. We didn't blink. It was like a staring contest. Dani told me her dog, Maggie, stares deep in your eyes for the same reason human beings hug. That's how I felt right then with this little bird. Hugged.

I'd always wanted a pet. A dog like Dani's or, even better, a kitten. But Sophie was allergic to animal fur.

"Do you want to be my pet?" I asked the robin.

He blinked and bobbed his head. Did that mean yes? I opened my lunch bag and broke off a piece of granola bar. I held it out to him. He tilted his head to the side, but he didn't come any nearer. So I dropped the granola in the grass, and he grabbed it right up with his beak, swallowing it. I fed him another piece, and another. Then I held a piece between my finger and thumb.

The bird was very still. So was I. He hopped a tiny bit closer. Was he going to peck me? Or bite me? Did birds even have teeth? I was scared, but I tried not to show it.

Hop, hop, grab! He took the food right out of my hand and hopped away as soon as the granola was his.

"I'm Cassidy," I said. "Hi." I reached out. I wanted to touch his feathers but he was a little too far away.

He tilted his head to the side.

If he was going to be my pet, he'd need a name. I could call him Robin, but that was too predictable. Maybe something silly, like Mr. Featherhead. Or Bob! Because of the way he bobbed his head.

"Bob?" I asked.

He hopped farther away.

"Okay, no. Mr. Featherhead?"

He hopped even farther away.

I stared at him. The missing piece in the circle around his eye made me think of a picture book from when I was little. *The Missing Piece* by Shel Silverstein. "Shel?" I asked. "Shel Silverstein?"

The bird hopped closer to me.

And closer.

And closer still.

My heart pounded. Then he pecked my hand with his beak. Not too hard. It didn't hurt. It was more like a greeting. As in, *Hello, nice to meet you.*

Wow!

"Nice to meet you, too, Shel Silverstein," I whispered.

Down the block, the first bell rang at school, startling me and reminding me that even though I was having a very sweet and strange and surprising interaction with a wild bird, Dani and Lucy were heading into Mrs. Kwon's class together. My heart sank.

Shel Silverstein rose into the air and flew in a circle, as if he knew I had to leave for school. I put my voice recorder in my backpack and zipped it up.

"I hope you find your family," I said to Shel Silverstein. I didn't want him to spend the day by himself. "You should go look for them."

I checked the front door. No Sophie. My sister was taking forever. I couldn't believe I'd missed Monday morning hang-out time. I made my deep-down secret wish, the one I would never dare say out loud.

Finally, Sophie dragged out, moving slowly. Her eyes were puffy. She said, "Sorry, Cass. Thanks for waiting."

I stood up. "It's okay. But let's go." I had to make it to my classroom before second bell. Mrs. Kwon said fifth graders should be responsible enough to get to school on time.

Mom came running out of the house, holding her keys, purse, coffee, and phone. Her white blouse didn't look crisp anymore. "Do you girls want a ride?"

"No, we'll run," Sophie said. "It's good exercise. Right, Cass?"

"Right."

Besides, by the time we buckled in and Mom waited in the drop-off line, we'd be late for sure. Sophie took longer than most people to do things like buckling up.

Mom kissed my forehead and said, "You're a good sister, Cassidy Sunshine." She climbed into her car and yelled out the window, "Love you! Have a great day!"

I liked Mom's nickname for me. And sometimes I really did feel like a good sister. But if anyone knew my deep-down secret wish, they might not think I was so sunshiny. Or so good.

Chapter Three

I made it to room 5A just as Mrs. Kwon was closing the door. We were allowed to choose fist bump, high five, or hug at the beginning and end of each day. I always chose hug so I could get a whiff of Mrs. Kwon's strawberry shampoo. Mrs. Kwon had shoulder-length, shiny dark hair and a big smile that made you want to smile, too. It was embarrassing to admit, but I loved school.

I hugged my teacher and stepped inside. I couldn't wait to slide into my seat next to Dani and tell her about Shel Silverstein.

I stopped short. Our room looked different.

"New seats," Mrs. Kwon reminded me, pointing to the back left corner.

Right. Friday she'd said she was rearranging desks because we'd all been too chatty. Dani and I had been two of the chattiest. Now Dani was in the front right, kitty-corner from Lucy. Rats!

Dani and I waved to each other and frowned.

I hung up my jacket and backpack in my cubby. As I walked to my new spot, I noticed that everyone had hot pink envelopes they were tucking away inside their desks. Maybe it was a birthday invitation. I wondered whose. But when I got to my desk, way back in the Sahara Desert, there was no pink envelope. I looked on my chair and on the floor. Nothing.

Eli Fleishman, my mortal enemy since kindergarten, had the desk next to mine. "Did you take my invitation?" I asked him.

"What invitation?"

"Never mind."

"You mean those pink things? They're coupons, not invitations. Lucy gave them out."

Coupons? That made no sense. Eli Fleishman didn't know anything. Lucy London was probably having a party and she wasn't inviting me. Which was totally against school rules. Not to mention rude. Not to mention, why would she do that? I looked inside my desk to see if someone had already put it away for me.

Nope.

Eli leaned in too close and said, "Hey! We're next-door neighbors at home *and* at school now. Do you think Mrs. Kwon did that on purpose?"

I doubted it, but I shrugged and said maybe. Eli didn't know he was my mortal enemy. In fact, he'd already asked me to marry him. Twice—once in kindergarten and again in third grade. Yuck.

Eli's bedroom window and mine were right across from each other. The only thing separating us was the robins' tree. That tree was pink in spring, green in summer, and gold in fall. The problem was winter, when the tree became a skeleton, and I had to make sure my blinds were closed. One night, I accidentally saw Eli in his Spiderman underwear. I didn't want that to ever happen again.

Mrs. Walker, our principal, came over the PA and said it was time for the Pledge of Allegiance, so we stood and faced the flag. I put my hand over my heart and said the right words, but all I thought about were those pink envelopes. I was being left out again. But this was worse than a two-person sleepover. It was the whole class! Why would Lucy London do that? I'm a nice person. Last year, at the end of fourth grade, we all had to write anonymous compliments to each other, and that was what almost everyone said. *Nice. Smiley. Helpful. Kind.* One person said I was cute, but I'm pretty sure that was Eli, so: blech. The point was, I was not the kind of person who would be left out of a whole class party. Not that *anyone* should be left out of a whole class party!

Unless….

Maybe it was a mistake. It could have been a mistake. Yes, it had to be a mistake.

I sighed. Lucy London took a lot of energy.

After the Pledge ended but before we could sit down, Mrs. Kwon announced, "Bakiwang says…"

Happy sounds bounced around our classroom. We all loved Bakiwang Says, which was like Simon Says, only really advanced. Plus, Bakiwang was the Queen of the Earth in Korean mythology, as opposed to Simon, who was just some bossy guy.

"Bakiwang says face east," Mrs. Kwon said in her special rumbly Bakiwang voice.

At the beginning of the year, I had no idea which way was east in our classroom. I thought east was always on my right, the way it was on a map, but now I knew east didn't change no matter where you were. East was always east. And east in room 5A was the wall of windows.

I turned there quickly. So did everyone except Eli, who turned west.

Mrs. Kwon gave him the "sit down" nod, and he slumped in his seat. "It's confusing sitting in a new spot," he mumbled.

We kept playing, and Mrs. Kwon made it harder and harder, but I pictured myself looking at a map, and I got everything right. Downtown Chicago—south, the whiteboard. Where the sun sets—west, the door to the hallway. Wisconsin—north, the cubbies. I was a geography master! Mrs. Kwon did a fast bunch of orders in a row: Bakiwang says face California. Bakiwang says about face. Left face. She was speaking so fast that a bunch of kids kept moving even when she didn't say Bakiwang says first. Soon there were only five of us left. Then three. Then two.

Lucy and me.

The class cheered for us every time we got an answer right.

16

My pulse raced. I liked being in the final round, and I especially liked being in it with Lucy London. Maybe this would help her see I was somebody she should be friends with—not somebody to leave out.

Mrs. Kwon raised one eyebrow in a way that meant she was about to give us a really tough one. "Bakiwang says face your house."

Tricky because Lucy and I didn't live near each other. In fact, I wasn't sure where Lucy lived because she took the bus to school and I wasn't at the sleepover. Our house was right down the street, so I faced the window but angled myself a little north. Lucy hesitated for a moment, confused. Then she faced the same direction as me.

Mrs. Kwon pulled up a map of our neighborhood and projected it onto the whiteboard. She asked us both for our addresses. I gave her mine, and she circled my house on the map. "Class, is Cassidy's house northeast of our room?"

"Yes!"

"Bakiwang says correct!"

YES!!

Then Lucy gave her address, and Mrs. Kwon circled her house on the map. It was on the other side of school, over the railroad tracks and in the middle of the downtown area, next to the fountain. I could see right away it wasn't northeast of our room. So could Lucy.

She said, "No fair! Cassidy lives right down the street."

She was right. It wasn't very fair. I gave her a sad smile, but she didn't return it. Lucy slumped in her chair.

Mrs. Kwon pointed to the sign on the bulletin board that had an X through the word whining. Then she said, "Congratulations, Cassidy. You're our Bakiwang Says champ! A round of applause."

I wanted to feel happy about my win, but it was hard when

Lucy was so mad. It was like she'd taken all the fizz out of my pop.

Still, I smiled and raised my arms in victory as the class clapped their hands in circles. Get it? A *round* of applause? I loved Mrs. Kwon.

"Come on up and get your prize," Mrs. Kwon said, opening her box of trinkets from South Korea. You never knew when you'd get to choose a prize from Mrs. Kwon's box. Could be for anything from winning Bakiwang Says to getting the highest grade on a test to doing a random act of kindness. I'd already gotten a key chain with a bunny face that I'd clipped to my backpack, a prize for helping Eli with fractions. I thought about picking another keychain. There were so many cute ones, and it would be fun to have them clanging together on my backpack, but maybe that would be braggy. So instead, I chose a bright pair of Sailor Moon socks.

As I walked back to my desk, Mrs. Kwon said, "We're going to use more of our map skills for the next assignment." She held up a stack of maps of the United States. "You can pick your own partners and work together to fill in these maps with the state names and capitals."

I looked across the rows of desks to catch eyes with Dani. We were always partners when we got to choose. But Lucy had already grabbed Dani's hand. Dani looked over at me, checking, I guess, if it was okay. It wasn't okay. Not at all.

Here's what I wanted to do: Tell Lucy London to back off!

Here's what I actually did: I gave Dani a thumbs-up.

I mean, it's not like I would start a fight over something as silly as partners for one assignment. I was not a fight-starting kind of girl. Besides, I still wanted Lucy to invite me to her party. I wanted all three of us to be friends. Starting a fight was not the way to make that happen.

Eli tapped me on the arm. "Hey, neighbor, wanna be partners?"

18

I definitely did not want to be partners with Eli Fleishman. Besides the fact that he was my secret mortal enemy, he also had the worst handwriting, and he didn't know any of the capitals. He even thought Chicago was the capital of Illinois! But everyone else was already pairing up, and I knew nobody would want to work with Eli, so I said okay.

Chapter Four

The bell rang for lunch, and we went to our cubbies. Mine was right next to Lucy London's, which I'd thought was lucky on the first day of school. I pulled my brown paper bag out of my backpack. If Lucy meant to invite me to her party, I figured she'd mention something about it while we stood together. Like, *Hey, are you coming to my party?* But if she didn't mention the party, it would mean she really and truly wanted to leave me out.

She rummaged through her backpack, which was white and looked brand new, even though we'd been at school since the end of August.

I said, "That last Bakiwang Says question was totally unfair."

"Yeah, it was. You beat me, though."

I shrugged. "It was kind of more like a tie. But it's such a fun game. I love how Mrs. Kwon makes school feel like a *party* sometimes."

"Yeah, she's great."

I waited patiently, but she didn't get the hint. She didn't say anything about her party. Which meant she really wasn't going to invite me.

I'd never had to try so hard to make a new friend. All my friendships had just...happened. But Lucy was tricky to figure out. Sometimes she was nice to me, but other times she acted like I was taking up space for no good reason.

In September, Mrs. Diamond, our music teacher, had asked everyone who wanted the solo for our fifth-grade fall assembly to sing in front of the class. Lucy had a good voice, and I was sure she was going to get it, especially since she was new this year, but Mrs. Diamond gave the role to me. That's when I first started getting the feeling Lucy London didn't like me so much.

I thought about that and also how I'd won Bakiwang Says. Maybe Lucy London was jealous of me? Rats.

"Do you want my prize?" I asked her. "They're Sailor Moon socks. You can have them."

"Why would I take your prize?"

"Well, because. That last question. And…"

"I don't even like *Sailor Moon.*"

"Oh. Okay." Why did it feel like she was saying she didn't like *me*?

She got her lunch from her backpack. It was in a black-and-white-checkered lunchbox. Maybe I should get a lunchbox instead of using a brown paper bag.

I hated how Lucy made me feel so unsure of everything.

"Hey!" Dani said, coming up between us. "Did you see the brochure?" she asked me. "I'm taking hip-hop."

Huh? "What brochure?"

"The one from Lucy. Her mom's dance studio."

I was still confused.

"In the pink envelope."

"Oh!" Relief rushed through me. "I thought that was a party invitation."

"Party?" Lucy asked. "How can you confuse a brochure and a coupon for a party invitation?"

"Um, because I didn't get one."

"You didn't? Oh, whoops. I put them on everyone's desks," Lucy said. "Even the boys. I must have missed yours." She dug in her backpack and pulled out another pink envelope. "It was hiding at the bottom, I guess. Sorry."

She handed it to me. But before she let go, she said, "You thought I was having a party and inviting the whole class except for you?"

The way she said it made me sound like a baby. Pitiful and insecure.

21

"No. Not really."

"I would never do that," she said. "I'm not mean." She said it like I'd accused her of being mean, which I hadn't. At least not out loud.

"I know," I said, even though I didn't quite, one-hundred percent, know that for sure. "I was just confused."

Dani said, "Nobody's mean! But open it, Cass. It's so cool. Lucy's mom owns a dance studio, and they live upstairs!"

Lucy smiled at Dani. Then she explained to me, "We had a studio in Manhattan before we moved here, so this is like no big deal. But my mom wanted me to hand these out so all my new friends could get a discount. Sort of embarrassing, to tell the truth."

"Wow, that is cool," I said, acting excited.

I hadn't meant to hurt her feelings. And who knew? Maybe it was sort of cool. The studio was called Fusion Two, and I recognized Lucy in one of the pictures on the front of the brochure. Her long, shiny black ponytail was impossible to miss. I wondered if the other dancers in the photos were her friends from New York. It was weird thinking about Lucy before she moved here. Like she'd had this whole life that we weren't a part of, and now all of a sudden, she was here in our world.

"Girls," Mrs. Kwon said. "Lunch?"

I stuck the brochure and coupon in my backpack and we headed into the crowded hall.

Dani said, "So, hip-hop. My mom already said okay. You have to take it, too, Cass."

"Hip-hop would be fun," I said. I hoped my parents would say yes.

Lucy's ponytail swung as we walked down the hall. I wondered how she got it to be so shiny and swingy.

Dani said, "You'll love it. Sharon gave us a mini lesson on Saturday. She's a great teacher."

"Sharon?"

"My mom," Lucy said.

"Oh."

Dani called my parents Mr. and Mrs. Carlson. I pictured this Sharon person in dance pants and probably a crop top, doing hip-hop with Dani and Lucy. I felt a flash of jealousy. But that was dumb. I had to stop thinking of Lucy as an intruder. We could all be friends. Maybe I would get to meet Sharon at a sleepover at Lucy's soon. Or at dance class. I really hoped I could go.

"Why is there always a drawing of a sun on your lunch?" Lucy asked me.

I looked at the sketch on my lunch bag. I hardly paid attention to that sun anymore. Mom had been drawing it for as long as I could remember. I didn't want to tell Lucy my nickname. She might think being called Cassidy Sunshine was babyish. "My mom just likes to draw suns, I guess."

"Weird," Lucy said.

"Totally," I said.

Dani didn't say anything, but she raised one eyebrow at me.

❧

The lunchroom was actually the school gym. Each class sat at their own long table, and we had unofficial assigned seats. Basically, wherever we ended up sitting on the first day of school was where we sat for the rest of the year. My spot was at the end, next to Dani's. Lucy sat across from us. The rest of the girls in our class filled in our end of the table. The boys sat on the other end.

The conversation, as we unpacked our lunches, was all about Fusion Two. They all suddenly wanted to be dancers.

It was the Lucy-factor.

"Hip-hop's on Wednesdays," Lucy said. "You should all take it."

Wednesdays? Oh no.

"Darn! I have Hebrew school," Shayna said.

"I have basketball." Holly frowned.

"Stinks for you," Lucy said. She stuck out her tongue and crossed her eyes, and everybody laughed.

All the other girls said they'd ask their parents. So did I. Even though I already knew there was a problem.

I bit into my bagel and cream cheese. I had voice lessons on Wednesdays. The best part of my week. But maybe, hopefully, Javier could switch me to another day.

❧

After lunch I went with all the girls to our regular spot at the top of the jungle gym dome. We always started off recess there, then we'd think of something fun to do. I climbed to the top and looked out across the playground. The fourth, fifth, and sixth graders had recess at the same time, so I kept an eye on Sophie. Her aide helped her in class but not during recess. Sophie liked to hang out with two fourth-grade girls. They were sitting under their usual tree, trading Pokémon cards.

A cool breeze blew, and Shel Silverstein swooped past us. At least I thought it was him. Birds looked a lot alike. I tried to get a peek at his eyes, but he was a whir of motion.

"Who wants to play crack the whip?" Lucy asked. "Me and my friends used to play it on skates at Rockefeller Center, but it's fun on the playground too."

"I'll play," I said, even though I wasn't sure what crack the whip was. Or Rockefeller Center, for that matter. But Lucy was great at coming up with new things for us to do at recess.

Everyone else was in, too, so we all jumped down from the dome.

The robin came back and flew near me, and I was able to spot the missing piece in the circle around his eye. Shel Silverstein had followed me to school.

He really was my pet!

"Okay, line up," Lucy said. "I'll be the leader because I'm the tallest."

Shel Silverstein swooped in even closer.

"What's up with that robin?" Lucy said. "He's like an attack bird or something."

"No, he's not," I said. And then, before I could think it through, I added, "He's my pet."

Lucy raised one eyebrow. "You have a pet robin?"

"Yes," I said. "Kind of."

Dani laughed and said, "Cass! You do not!"

"I do. I just met him this morning, but I've sort of known him for a while. His name is Shel Silverstein."

Everyone laughed at that. Shel Silverstein landed on the top of the dome and watched us.

"He talks?" Lucy asked. "He told you his name?"

"Of course not! I named him. Because of his eye. See?" I pointed. "It has a missing piece."

Lucy looked confused.

"Didn't you read that book when you were younger?" I asked her. "*The Missing Piece?* About the circle looking for the wedge that was missing from his body?"

She shook her head, like I had a missing piece of my brain.

"Mrs. Pelling read that story to us in kindergarten," Dani said.

"Right," I said. "And Shel Silverstein's the author. He wrote *The Giving Tree* book too. You must know that one."

"The one about the tree that turns into a stump after it gives everything away?" Lucy asked.

"Well, it's kind of about love and taking care of people, too, but yeah, that's the one."

"I hated that book," Lucy said.

Sailor Moon and *The Giving Tree*. Lucy sure was picky.

"Anyway," I said. "That's the bird's name. Shel Silverstein."

"That's a perfect name," Dani said. "So funny. And cool that you have a pet bird now!"

"Not really," Lucy said. "Birds carry disease."

"They do?" I asked.

"Of course. And you can't have a wild animal as a pet. If wild animals come near humans, it's usually because they're sick or something."

Uh-oh. What if that was why Shel Silverstein was following me? Maybe he didn't want to be my pet. Maybe he needed help.

Shel Silverstein flew off the dome and circled over our heads.

"Watch out!" Lucy shouted. "We're all gonna get pooped on!" Then she ran like she was being chased by a monster, and everyone followed her, laughing. "Rabies bird! Rabies bird!" she shouted.

I didn't think birds could have rabies. And I didn't like the way Lucy was making fun of poor Shel Silverstein. Besides, he didn't seem sick to me. He seemed lonely.

I stood there for a second, not knowing what to do. But Dani and all my friends were running away from the bird. And away from me. So I shooed Shel Silverstein and said, "Go find your family. You need to be with your bird friends while I'm at school."

Shel Silverstein flew over to a nearby tree and landed on a branch. He crouched down and tucked his wings in. He stared at me stubbornly, as if to say, *I'm not moving.*

That bird! I ran and caught up to my friends.

"Okay, Cassidy Bird Whisperer," Lucy said to me. "You can be the tail of the whip because you're the shortest." She leaned in and whispered, "That's the most fun spot. It's a prize from me to you for winning Bakiwang Says. Better than Sailor Moon socks."

"Cool," I said, shoving my bad feelings about Lucy's teasing into my junk drawer.

She said to everyone else, "Get in height order and hold hands."

Dani was right next to me. She was only one inch taller. I held her hand. She squeezed, and I didn't know why but that one little squeeze made me think everything would be okay. Dani was my best friend, and that's what really mattered.

As soon as everyone got in place, Lucy took off, ponytail swinging. Soon Dani got jerked forward, and her hand almost slipped out of mine. I gripped tighter, and we ran all over the playground, past kids playing wall-ball and others playing kickball and others on the swings and jungle gym and monkey bars. We were all laughing and screaming. I zipped this way and that, totally out of breath. It was like I was in the last car of a roller coaster, the fastest, jerkiest spot. My feet were doing the best they could to keep up, but it wasn't easy. Maybe this was the most fun spot for Lucy London, but not so much for me and my shrimpy legs. All of a sudden, I tripped and went flying through the air.

Wham, I sprawled in a pile of wood chips.

Ow!!!

I sat up and tried to catch my breath.

My right ankle hurt, and my hands stung. I'd torn a small hole in the knee of my jeans, and my hands were scraped and a tiny bit bloody. I pressed them together. I wouldn't cry. I wouldn't.

Here's what I thought would happen next: Dani would come over and say, "Cass! Are you all right?" Then all the girls would gather around, and one or two of them would walk me to the nurse.

Here's what actually happened: Everyone just kept laughing and running like nothing was wrong. Only Shel Silverstein flitted over. He chirped and circled, circled and chirped.

But really, what could a bird do for me?

The girls were on the other side of the playground. They were winding their way toward me. I held my ankle and waited for someone to notice.

Around the twisty slide came Lucy London, hooting and laughing, with all the other girls behind her. She ran right past me and kept on going. They all did. Dani looked back and yelled, "Come on, Cass! Get up!" She held her hand out to me as if I could just hop up and join the fun. Didn't she realize I was hurt?

Suddenly, I felt lonely. Like the lonely I felt when Sophie was dysregulated and Mom and Dad were on their last nerve, and our house seemed like a place for four separate people instead of a family.

Mrs. T., the recess monitor, came over and asked if I was okay. My throat felt all clogged, but I told her I was fine.

"You sure?" she asked.

I nodded. Then I stood and brushed myself off, to prove I was fine, to her and to me. I even took a few steps and realized my ankle didn't hurt that much after all.

"Okay, honey," Mrs. T. said. "But you should go to the nurse to get cleaned up. You might need bandages for your hands. Do you want a friend to walk you there?"

I looked at all my friends running around the playground without me.

Even Sophie hadn't noticed I was hurt. What good was a big sister who didn't help you when you got hurt at recess? She was still under her bright red maple tree with her friends. I thought about calling her over, but what if she didn't want to stop what she was doing, and she got upset? Or what if she came with me and ended up talking nonstop to the nurse? And what if she touched too many things in the nurse's office and something broke? And then she started crying and couldn't stop?

"I'll go by myself," I said.

And that's exactly what I did.

Chapter Five

Every Monday after school, I went to Dani's because that was when Dad brought Sophie to her therapy appointment. Dani's mom was an artist, and she liked to go all out with holidays. Last year, they did an outer-space Halloween theme and got featured on the news. This year, it was going to be Halloween Down on the Farm, and Dani and I were going to build a vampire-scarecrow for their front yard. I was excited about the project, but even more excited to spend time with Dani away from Lucy London.

Dani's house was only a block and a half from school but in the opposite direction from mine. To get there, we had to walk down a path behind the playground. One time, in first grade, we went to Dani's house in the middle of recess because her mom had made brownies the day before and we wanted some. We knew we were doing something naughty. I mean, we definitely were sneaking off the playground, but we hadn't realized how bad that was until her mom answered the door and almost had a heart attack. Then she started speaking in really fast Spanish, and she grabbed both our hands and marched us back to school and straight into Mrs. Walker's office. That was the only time I saw Mrs. Martinez lose her patience. And to be clear, we did not get any brownies.

Today after school, we were walking down the path when I felt a breeze, and a shadow crossed over us. We both looked up at the same time and said, "Shel Silverstein!"

"That bird is actually following you," Dani said.

"I know! Do you think birds carry diseases?"

Dani shrugged. "Maybe the ones in New York do."

"This bird is so cute. I don't think he's sick." I told Dani what had happened that morning. "It's weird, right? That his family is gone, and he's following me around?"

"Definitely weird, but in the best way! It's like that *Are You My Mother?* book. He thinks you're his family now!"

We both laughed and waved to Shel Silverstein, who was flying overhead, zipping in front of us, landing on trees, then circling back. "I just hope his actual family is okay. I don't know where they went or what happened to them. I loved when they all sang together in the mornings. It was like I had my own personal concert to start each day."

"Well, maybe Shel Silverstein wants to be a solo performer," Dani said.

"Maybe." But I didn't think so. Shel Silverstein was lonely. I was worried about his family, and I hoped they'd be back soon.

We walked along in a comfortable silence. I considered asking Dani if she thought Lucy told me to be the tail of the whip because she knew I'd fall down. Or if she purposely didn't give me the dance coupon. Or if she faked the rule about a one-friend sleepover. But I knew Dani would say Lucy hadn't done any of that on purpose. She'd say I was being too sensitive. And maybe I was. Lucy London was an intruder only if I thought of her that way. Dani was my best friend and Lucy was someone new and we would all be friends soon enough.

I made sure my voice was perfectly normal when I asked, "How was your sleepover with Lucy?"

"Fun!"

I waited for her to say more, but that was it. Fun. That one word gave me an itchy feeling. So I couldn't help myself. My inside question came out. "Does Lucy have something against me?"

Dani stopped in her tracks. "What? No! Of course not. What makes you say that?"

"It's just a feeling I have. I know it's dumb. And insecure. Never mind."

"You guys just need to get to know each other better. That's why you have to take hip-hop with us on Wednesdays."

"But I have voice lessons on Wednesdays."

"Oh, shoot, I forgot."

How could she have forgotten that? I knew Dani's schedule: Tuesdays and Thursdays she had gymnastics. Wednesdays I went to voice and Mondays we hung out. Sometimes Fridays and Saturdays too.

"Can't you switch to a different day?" she asked.

"That's what I'm hoping," I said.

"Good, because I want all three of us to be best friends."

I hadn't put the word *best* in front of *friends* when I'd thought of the three of us. But I supposed I could get used to it. "That's what I want too," I said.

I wasn't sure that's what Lucy wanted though.

❧

"*Holá, Mami!* We're home!" Dani called from the foyer.

Dani's big yellow dog, Maggie, bounded over to us. Maggie had brought me her favorite toy, a raggedy old elephant. I took the elephant, which was only a little slobbery, and I scratched under Maggie's chin to say thank you.

Dani's little brother ran over, sliding into the foyer on mismatched socks. His hair was covered with white goop tucked under a shower cap. He smelled like mayonnaise, and he was sucking on a lollipop. "Guess what? I got bugs in my hair!"

"Cool," I said, even though it was really gross.

"Oh no!" Dani said.

Mrs. Martinez came into the foyer. She had on thin rubber gloves—the kind doctors wear, not the kind parents wear when they do dishes. All her hair was tucked away beneath a baseball hat. She held up her hands, blocking us from coming any farther. "Rafi got sent home from school with lice."

"So, no vampire-scarecrow?" Dani asked.

"Not today," Mrs. Martinez said. "Sorry, *niñas*. Do your heads itch?"

Mine didn't until she asked. Suddenly it did. Dani and I both started scratching.

Mrs. Martinez laughed. "*Dios mío*. Okay, Rafi, back to your movie. Girls, let me check you. Come into the good light."

We followed Dani's mom into their sunny living room. Mrs. Martinez checked my head first.

"How was your day?" she asked, going through my hair. It tickled in a nice way. I liked the way Mrs. Martinez was so calm even though Rafi, and possibly their whole house, was infested with lice.

"Good," I said.

Dani said, "We have new seats. I'm in the front row."

"That's nice," Mrs. Martinez said.

"No, it's not. I used to sit in the middle, next to Cass."

"Oh well; easy come, easy go," Mrs. Martinez said.

Sometimes parents made no sense at all. I scrunched my eyebrows at Dani, and she shrugged. She didn't know what her mom meant either.

"You are lice free, my dear," Mrs. Martinez said. "Dani, *mi hija*, you're up."

While she checked Dani's hair, I helped myself to jelly beans. We didn't have a lot of sugary treats at our house because they riled Sophie up, but at Dani's, there was a bowl of jelly beans that was always full. You didn't even have to ask before you took some.

After Mrs. Martinez declared us both lice free, she called Dad to see if we could go to our house instead. Rats! My house wasn't as fun as Dani's. Besides, Dad was taking Sophie to therapy. I knew he'd say no, and my plans with Dani would be over. Then Dani would call Lucy and make plans with her instead. I'd be left out again. I'd have to go to Sophie's therapy appointment and wait in the waiting room with Dad.

I ate a few handfuls of jelly beans and listened to Mrs. Martinez's side of the conversation. "Mm hm…*sí*…well, if it's not a problem…*sí, sí*…right, okay."

She hung up and said, "All right, *niñas*, Sophie has a doctor's appointment, so you'll tag along."

My mood lifted. Tagging along to Sophie's therapy appointment with Dani would be way more fun than tagging along by myself.

"Can't we just play outside here?" Dani asked.

"I can't supervise right now, Dani. I know it's not ideal, but this is a lice-is-crisis."

Dani said, "I hate doctors' offices. Especially the ones that smell funny. Does this one smell?" she asked me.

"Daniela!" Mrs. Martinez said.

I said, "That's okay, I know what she means. But this one doesn't smell." One time one of the moms there ate something weird and oniony from a plastic container, but I didn't tell Dani about that. She was already bummed enough. "It sort of smells like a library. Or school."

"Okay. That's not bad."

"And it's not really a doctor's office. It's a therapy office."

"What's the difference?"

"No white coats, no lollipops, no sick kids. And it's only an hour. While we wait we can do something fun…like make friendship bracelets for each other."

Dani smiled. "Great idea!"

❧

Shel Silverstein started following us the minute we left Dani's house. He must have been waiting outside for us.

"What's that song about the birds?" Dani asked. "You know, I've got so much sunshine, the birds envy me, or something like that?"

"I think it goes, 'I've got so much honey, the bees envy me,'" I sang.

Dani said, "I like my version better." Then she sang, "I've got Cassidy Sunshine so this bird envies me!" Dani didn't sing well, but that never stopped her.

Dani and I sang "I Got Sunshine," as we walked to my house, making up the words we couldn't remember and changing the ones we felt like changing.

Eli Fleishman was kneeling in his front yard with his older brother when we walked up. Trey was in sixth grade, like Sophie, but he didn't have a disability. He was just regular. The two of them were doing something with magnifying glasses and shovels.

Eli wiped his hand across his face, leaving a trail of dirt on his cheek. "Want to help?" he asked us. "We're making a museum exhibit called Dirt."

Dani raised her eyebrows at me. Boys.

"No, thank you." We hurried into my house.

As we kicked off our shoes, Dani said, "Remember when Eli Fleishman wanted to play Dirt with us?"

I laughed. "Remembering" something that happened a second ago was a joke we'd started by accident back in kindergarten. We had just finished playing Guess Who, and we were coloring, and I was thinking about one of the faces from the Guess Who game, and I said, "Remember when we played Guess Who?" Dani had laughed so hard. And for some reason, it was still funny.

"Remember when Rafi got lice?" I said, and we both cracked up.

We went into the kitchen and said hi to Sophie and Dad. Sophie was eating apple slices with soy-nut-butter, and Dad put out more for Dani and me.

"I like your pants, Mr. Carlson," Dani said, with a totally straight face.

Dad smiled and said thanks. He was wearing the pajama bottoms Sophie and I had bought him for his birthday—

34

blue with SpongeBob SquarePants all over them. Nothing embarrassed my dad. Nothing.

Sophie said, "The thing about coming to my appointment is that you have to wait in the waiting room. And you have to be quiet so you don't disturb any of the other kids or therapists."

"I know," I said.

"Well, you know, but Dani hasn't been before, so I'm being helpful."

"Thanks, Sophie." Dani wiped the soy-nut-butter off her apple slice. "We'll be quiet."

Dani was being patient with Sophie, which I appreciated. It wasn't easy coming to my house. Friends hardly ever got to play with just me. Sophie always liked to be included. And we never knew when my sister was going to lose her temper.

"I get to pick the music in the car," Sophie said. "Because it's my appointment. Right, Dad?"

Dad was reading something on his phone. He wasn't paying attention to us, but he said, "Right, Soph."

Right, Sophie. Yes, Sophie. Whatever you say, Sophie. Those were magic words because it meant that Sophie might stay calm.

"What's your favorite day of the week, Dani?" Sophie asked. "Mine's Saturday because we get to sleep late and there's no school. But Sundays are good, too, except then you know Monday's coming so it's not *as* good."

Dani played along. "I don't know. Fridays, I guess."

"That's a popular one," Sophie said. "Thank god it's Friday and all. We did a survey in math today, and Friday came in second. Saturday was first. Cass's favorite day is Wednesday. Right, Cass? Because of Ja-vi-eeeer." She drew out the name and rolled her r's, pronouncing Javier's name as if I had a crush on him.

For the record, I didn't have a crush on Javier. I just loved him. And I loved singing. "Not because of Javier," I said, pronouncing his name normally. "But, yes."

35

"Don't forget to ask about hip-hop," Dani said.

Oh yeah, right. "Dad?"

He looked up from his phone.

"Do you think Javier can switch me to another day?"

"Why?"

"Because everyone is going to take hip-hop from Lucy's mom on Wednesdays, and I really, really, really want to too." I got up from the table and hugged him. "Plus there's a coupon. Twenty percent off. Please?"

Dad kissed my forehead. "Voice lessons are right near Sophie's OT appointment, so I can't change one without changing the other, and that would be tricky. Plus, I don't think we can afford another after-school activity, Cass, even with a coupon. You'll have to choose. Singing or dance."

I pulled away from Dad and glanced at Dani. She looked away from me and took a bite of her apple slice. Just because nothing embarrassed my dad didn't mean nothing embarrassed me.

I'd heard Dad say Sophie's medicine and therapy cost an arm and a leg. We didn't go on family vacations like Dani did, and I mostly wore hand-me-downs. Still, Dad didn't have to say that in front of my best friend.

Here's what I wanted to say to Dad: Sophie goes to karate and regular therapy and occupational therapy. That's three activities. I'm only asking for two.

Here's what I actually said: "Okay."

Because, really, I was not a brat.

I sat back down at the table even though I wasn't hungry anymore.

Dani said, "You're gonna pick hip-hop, right?"

I shrugged.

Sophie said, "No, she won't. She loves Ja-vi-eeeer." Again with his name.

"I love singing!"

"Okay, okay," Sophie said. "You are a great singer."

"That's true," Dani said. "You're gonna be a star someday."

My cheeks got hot. "Thanks."

"But you don't love Javier as much as you love me!" Dani said. "And dance is so much fun! I seriously had the best time, and it was only a mini-lesson. It's so cool. I think I like it even more than gymnastics. You're going to love it, I promise."

"Maybe," I said.

If I didn't take hip-hop, Lucy and Dani would be together without me every Wednesday. But if I did take hip-hop, I'd have to quit voice. If Lucy London weren't in the picture, I wouldn't even consider quitting voice, no matter how much I loved Dani.

I hated the Lucy-factor!

"Besides," Dani said, "a real star needs to be a triple threat. Singing, dancing, and acting. And you already can sing. So you should take hip-hop."

That kind of made sense. Maybe I needed to learn how to dance.

"I'll think about it," I said.

"Yay!" Dani for sure thought I was choosing dance.

"Dad," Sophie said. "Can you teach me to make fried eggs? I want to be more self-reliant in the mornings."

Dad smiled. "I love the idea of you being more self-reliant, kiddo. But we don't have time for a cooking lesson right now. In fact, we gotta go. You girls can take your snacks in the car if you haven't finished." He grabbed his keys from the counter.

"Dad," I said. "Um. Your pants?"

He looked down at himself, surprised. Then he said, "I'll just be a minute," before heading upstairs to change.

"Remember when your dad almost left the house in SpongeBob SquarePants pants?" Dani said.

The three of us shook our heads and laughed.

Chapter Six

In the waiting room, one mom was knitting a hat while another sat with a squirming boy who looked like he didn't want to be there. Luckily, nobody was eating anything oniony.

Dad signed in Sophie with the receptionist while my sister showed us where the kids' magazines were and which were the best chairs to sit on. "This is the sound machine," she said, pointing to a little box on the floor that made a gentle shushing noise like ocean waves. "It helps for privacy."

"That's cool," Dani said.

Sophie felt important, I could tell. It was like this was her place, and she was proud of it.

We sat on chairs near the door, across from the other people.

"Can we make the bracelets now?" Dani asked.

"Sure." I opened the box of string I'd brought with me and balanced it on my lap. It was stuffed with foot-long pieces of string in a variety of colors. Blue, red, yellow, pink, green....

"Oh, you're making bracelets?" Sophie asked. "Can I make one too?"

Tying knots wasn't easy for Sophie. Trying to make a bracelet would frustrate her for sure. I looked at Dad. He was busy on his phone. "I don't think you'll have time," I said.

"I can start one."

That was true. I let her pick out several pieces of string. Dani and I chose pink, yellow, and green, our favorite colors, and started tying knots. Sophie took the box of string from me and sat on the floor with it, going through the colors again and narrating as she went. "Blue is good, but this light blue is maybe prettier than the dark blue. Or there's a greenish blue, too. Or maybe this purple one. It's not my favorite, though."

I wished Sophie would keep her thoughts inside her brain and just choose some colors. I always felt more self-conscious about Sophie's odd behaviors, like talking too much, when we were in front of other people. I got embarrassed, even when it was my best friend.

Sophie kept voicing her thoughts while the boy went through the door to the office for his appointment, and his mom opened a magazine. The knitting mom kept knitting. Dad stayed on his phone. He had his work face on—pursed lips and a wrinkly forehead. Finally, Sophie's therapist opened the door and called her in.

Sophie didn't look up from the box of string. "I'm making an important decision," she said. "Can you hold on?"

Dad put his phone away. "Soph, you can do that later. Debra asked you to come in for your session."

"Just a minute," Sophie said.

Debra came over and bent down. "That's a lot of pretty string."

"Yes, I'm making a bracelet." She did not take her eyes off the string.

"That sounds like fun, but this is our special time together, so maybe you can do that afterwards."

"No! I need to choose my colors now."

Need. Not want. This meant trouble. I could see the fight collecting in Sophie's body.

One time, about two years ago, Dani was sleeping at my house. Normally, I only had a friend over if Sophie did too, because it was hard for Sophie to share me with other people. That time, though, Sophie's friend had canceled at the last minute. Mom had asked if I wanted to reschedule my sleepover or if I wanted to go to Dani's house instead, but I said no because I always went to Dani's. At the time, Sophie had been doing really well. She'd started a new medicine, and it seemed like maybe we had nothing to worry about.

39

But I should have worried.

Sophie wanted to do everything with us, which was okay when we made Shrinky-Dinks and sang karaoke and watched a movie and ate pizza and popcorn. But after Dani and I rolled out sleeping bags on the rug in my room, Sophie begged to sleep with us.

"There's not enough room," I said.

"Yes, there is."

"This is the sleeping part, not the playing part," I said.

"So? I need to sleep too."

"We might want to talk about private things," I said.

"You can't keep secrets from me! That's not nice!"

"Mom!" I called.

Mom came up, and I told her we wanted the sleeping part of the sleepover to be just us. Mom told Sophie she had to sleep in her own room.

That's when Sophie said, "But I *need* to sleep with them." Then her face scrunched up and turned red. Her body tightened.

She wailed louder than the lightning warning siren at school.

Dani's eyes went wide. Even though she knew Sophie got extra help for some of her issues, she'd never seen her totally dysregulated. She'd never seen a Super Sophie Tantrum. I could tell Dani was surprised, but the scary part hadn't even happened yet. When Sophie cried, she went from sad to mad before you had time to hand her a tissue. Sad Sophie might be surprising, but mad Sophie was something else. She could be downright frightening. She sometimes kicked and hit and swore and broke things. Usually, I hid in my room until it ended.

I worried Dani might never come to my house again.

Thankfully, Mom took over. She picked up Sophie, which wasn't easy to do when she was out of control, and carried her out. Mom took my sister into her own room so she could finish her tantrum there.

I turned on music super loud. I pretended everything was fine. Dani pretended, too, but not that everything was fine. She said she had a stomachache, and she called her mom. Then she packed her overnight bag and rolled up her sleeping bag, and we waited together downstairs. I said, "Remember when Sophie freaked out at our sleepover?" but Dani didn't laugh.

We stood there and looked out the front window, trying to ignore the sounds of Sophie yelling upstairs. Finally, Mrs. Martinez's minivan's headlights swept into our house.

"I hope you feel better," I said.

She said, "Thanks. Sorry. I must have eaten too much popcorn."

And then she left.

That was the first time I made my deep-down secret wish.

And it was the last time Dani saw Sophie out of control. I worried she was about to see it happen again.

Here's what I thought would happen next: Sophie would throw a Super Sophie Tantrum, and Dani would be so upset that she wouldn't want to make plans with me anymore. She'd ditch me for Lucy London, and the two of them would hip-hop into the sunset.

Here's what actually happened: I became Cassidy Sunshine, sister extraordinaire.

I said, "I'll make a bracelet for you, Soph. You'll have it when you come out. And the colors will be a surprise!"

"That's sweet of you," Debra said.

Sophie smiled. "Okay. Because we're friends, not just sisters. Right, Cass?"

"Right."

Sophie left the waiting room with Debra. I said to Dani, "You don't mind if I give this bracelet to Sophie, do you?"

"Oh," Dani said. "But those are our favorite colors."

"Good point." I picked out some new colors. Two blues and a purple.

Then Dani said, "I thought you were making a bracelet for me."

"Well, I have to make one for Sophie."

Dani bit her lower lip. "You don't *have* to."

"Yes, I do." Dani frowned and looked away. "What?" I asked.

"Nothing. Never mind." Dani tossed her string back in the box and chose new colors.

"What are you doing?" I asked.

"I might as well make one for someone else too."

My stomach dropped. "Who?" But I knew. I already knew.

"I don't know. Lucy, I guess."

Jealousy flooded my heart. This wasn't the three of us being best friends. This was Dani replacing me with Lucy London.

Dani bent her head over her string. Her wavy brown hair hid her face.

The ocean waves from the sound machine seemed louder, like they were filling up the whole room.

"Okay, fine," I said, thinking it was anything but fine. I concentrated on my string.

Dani didn't say a word, and the two of us sat there, tying knots in friendship bracelets for other people.

After a while, Dani whispered, "Is Sophie going to grow out of her...stuff?"

I shrugged. "I don't know."

"She doesn't have autism, though. Right?"

It was hard to explain Sophie's disability. She had a sensory processing disorder. And she also had emotional issues, coordination problems, and other challenges. But she was pretty good at communicating. Sophie was just Sophie. Nobody, not even my best friend, really understood because it was so unusual. Especially since Sophie looked and acted like a regular kid a lot of the time.

But at that moment, I didn't want to try to explain any of that to Dani. So all I said was, "Right."

42

Chapter Seven

That night, I made a list:

REASONS TO TAKE HIP-HOP:

1. Dani and Lucy and everyone else will be taking it, and if I don't take hip-hop, Dani and Lucy will probably for sure become best friends and forget all about me.

2. If I want to be a triple threat, I should learn how to dance.

3. It would be fun to learn something new.

4. There will probably be a dance recital. Maybe on a real stage!!

REASONS TO STICK WITH VOICE:

1. Javier says I have "bee-yoo-tee-fool" tone!

2. The practice room walls are covered in old album covers, and I don't know them all yet. They are very cool to look at.

3. Singing gives me a bubbly feeling inside.

4. When I sang the solo at our fifth-grade fall assembly last week, I wasn't scared (once I got started) even though I was singing in front of a whole gym full of people. Congrats to me!

5. When Dad posted my song online, a ton of people liked it and made really nice comments, and that felt amazing!

6. Javier does a year-end showcase for all his students and I'll get to perform. I could be a star!

7. Maybe someday I will be a professional singer. ☺

The list for voice was longer than the list for dance, so it should have been an easy decision: stick with voice. But it didn't feel easy to me. I put the list under my pillow and told myself to dream the right choice.

It was hard to fall asleep. Besides the hip-hop/voice and Dani/Lucy problems, I kept worrying about Shel Silverstein. I hoped he would find his family. What if he was all alone in the world?

When I woke up the next morning, I remembered my dream: I was at the beach with my family, and Sophie and I were digging a hole in the sand. Mom and Dad kept saying it needed to be bigger so there would be room for all the pudding.

That didn't give me any answers. It didn't even make sense.

I jumped out of bed and pulled up the blinds. Shel Silverstein sat in the robins' tree, all alone. Rats!

I opened my window. "Good morning, Shel Silverstein! I guess you didn't find your family yesterday."

He chirped and flew about in a frenzy. I wished I could speak bird so I'd know what he was saying.

The bird feeder was empty. "You're hungry," I said. "I can fix that."

I closed the window and got dressed. Then I woke up Sophie and ran down to the kitchen.

"Making breakfast yourself again, Sunshine?" Mom asked me.

"Actually, could you make it for me? I have to fill the bird feeder."

Mom took eggs, milk, and butter out of the fridge. "You know, honey, I'm not sure we need to keep filling the bird feeder this time of year. Most of the birds are flying south for the winter. You'll just be feeding the squirrels."

My heart skipped a beat. Oh no. What if Shel Silverstein's family had already flown south and accidentally left him behind? Like *Home Alone* but with birds!

I told Mom, "But there's a robin out there. I saw him this morning."

"Sounds like a straggler," Mom said. "Which reminds me…" She called upstairs for Sophie to hurry up.

I opened the bag of birdseed and scooped some into a bowl. "Not every bird goes south for the winter, do they?"

"Most of the robins around here do. It's hard for them to find enough food and water in the winter."

The knot of worry grew inside my belly. Poor Shel Silverstein! He really was all alone. And winter was coming.

❧

I moved the stepladder we kept on the side of the house over to the robins' tree. Then I climbed up.

Shel Silverstein watched as I poured the seeds from the bowl into his feeder. He pecked at the food, eating all the raisins first.

I said, "You like raisins best, huh? I can bring you more tomorrow."

He stared at me with his beady black eyes.

I said, "Um, Shel Silverstein, did your family maybe fly south for the winter?"

I didn't know why I expected him to answer. He was a bird! And a hungry bird, at that. He returned to his peck-peck-pecking.

From my perch on the ladder, I was able to see across the street, where a couple of blue jays sat on a branch, squawking. That gave me an idea. I said, "Do you know those jays?"

Shel Silverstein looked up.

"The ones across the street. They seem nice."

Shel Silverstein ruffled his feathers and went back to eating.

"I'm just saying, while I'm at school, you might want to make friends with some other birds, so you won't be lonely."

Shel Silverstein looked at me and cocked his head. It felt like he was telling me, *I would never be friends with those jays!*

True, the birds were quite different. The jays were dark blue and black and white, and they made squawky noises and loud piercing calls. The robins chirped and sang so sweetly. Still, they were all birds.

"They're not so bad," I said to Shel Silverstein.

It was strange that I believed we understood each other. But

Shel Silverstein was not a normal bird. There was something magical about him. We had a kind of connection. I wished I could bring him into our home. Get a birdcage and keep him in my room. But that didn't feel right. It seemed mean, unfair. A bird had to fly.

Not to mention, I was sure Mom and Dad would veto bringing a wild bird into our house. Even if the bird behaved like he wanted to be my pet. Even if his family had flown south without him.

"Oh, Shel Silverstein." My heart squeezed. I didn't know what else to say. We stared at each other. I got that hugging feeling again. It made me close my eyes and take a deep breath.

Mom opened the back door and called me in for breakfast.

"I'll see you after school," I said to my bird. "And maybe at recess."

Then I thought about Lucy London. "Actually, it's better if you don't come too close at recess. You should make friends with those jays. Really. I bet they'd love you. Bye, Shel Silverstein!"

☙

Mom's french toast was delicious, but between the extra time I'd spent with Shel Silverstein and Sophie not being able to find the beret she said she needed to complete her outfit—polka-dot leggings and a fringed top—I wasn't able to get to school when I wanted. We ended up arriving after first bell again. Another morning of Dani and Lucy hanging out without me. Maybe it was for the best, though, because I didn't have to witness Dani giving Lucy the friendship bracelet she'd made at the therapy waiting room. Lucy made sure I saw it by swinging her arm all around, showing it off to everyone in our class.

At recess, the group of girls on top of the dome was much larger than usual. It was no longer just the girls in our class; now there were girls from the other fifth-grade classes too. I looked around the playground, first checking on Sophie, then searching for Shel Silverstein. A bird was perched in a tree in the distance, but it was too far away for me to tell.

Lucy said, "So who's coming to hip-hop tomorrow?"

"Me!" Dani shouted.

Lucy high-fived her.

"Me too!" a few of the other girls said.

More high-fives.

Evie said, "I'm almost for sure going."

"Almost?" Lucy said. "Why only almost?"

"I have an orthodontist appointment that my mom's trying to change."

Lucy put her hand up to high-five, but just as Evie was about to slap, Lucy pulled her hand away and said, "Then you only *almost* get a high five."

Monique said, "Oooh, shade!"

Evie laughed. We all did. But I felt my turkey sandwich from lunch twisting in my stomach.

Practically everyone else said they were going.

Lucy said, "What about you, Cass? You're being awfully quiet."

My heart was pounding, as if I felt scared. But why? I could tell Lucy London the truth.

Here's what I planned to say: I haven't decided yet.

Here's what actually came out of my mouth: "I'm going to hip-hop!"

Lucy gave me a high five.

Dani did too. Then she put her arm around my shoulder and squeezed, and in that moment, it felt like everything was good, and I'd made the right decision.

Chapter Eight

After school, Sophie started working on her latest fashion experiment—cutting up a skort to turn it into a top. Dad was in his office with a client emergency, Mom was still at work, and I had nothing to do.

I sat at the kitchen table and stared out the window while I ate a vanilla yogurt. I hadn't seen Shel Silverstein on our walk home from school, which worried me a little. Without a flock, who knew what kind of dangers he would face on his own? I hoped his family had realized they left him behind and returned for him. Shel Silverstein could be on his way to Florida at that very moment, but I had no way of knowing.

Usually when we got home from school on a Tuesday, Dad would make us do homework. After I finished, I'd go up to my room with my voice recorder and practice for my singing lesson on Wednesday. But there wasn't going to be a voice lesson tomorrow.

I licked the spoon and thought about how I'd begged Mom and Dad to let me take voice lessons. We had to apply for a scholarship, and I'd written an essay for the application, explaining why I loved to sing. I wrote about the bubbly feeling it gave me inside, even when bad stuff was happening. Then one night at the end of the summer while I was reading in bed, Mom and Dad came into my room. Mom handed me a small, beautifully wrapped box. We weren't the kind of family that gave presents for no reason, and it wasn't my birthday or Hanukkah, so I was confused.

"Open it," they said, and I could tell they were super excited.

I ripped off the shiny silver paper and saw it was a voice recorder. That's when they told me my scholarship had been approved. The money didn't make the lessons free, but it made them affordable. I wrapped my arms around Mom and Dad, and they hugged me tight, making a Cassidy sandwich.

I was nervous about starting the lessons. What if I wasn't good enough? What if the teacher was mean? But as soon as I walked in the practice room and met Javier, all my worries floated away. Javier taught me about folk-rock singers, and he introduced me to Ruby Maguire's music.

I wondered if hip-hop would be the same, or if it would be harder than singing. I imagined Lucy London's eyes in the mirror, watching me, judging me. My stomach tightened. But she'd probably be looking at herself more than me, anyhow. And Dani would be there. And lots of other kids from school.

I hadn't told Mom and Dad that I was quitting voice. I hoped they wouldn't be mad about the money they'd wasted on the voice recorder. Although it wasn't really wasted. I could still use it. In fact, I could still sing as much as I wanted. So what if I didn't take voice lessons? I could still practice.

I tossed my yogurt container in the recycling bin and took my voice recorder to the backyard. Our yard wasn't that big. Just a rectangle of grass, with bushes that separated our yard from our neighbors. The best thing out there was the oak tree in the middle. It was huge with lots of twisty branches. In the autumn it had orangey-brown leaves. Some of them were already falling, making pretty patterns on the lawn.

A couple of squirrels scampered up the tree as I crunched through the dead leaves and acorns covering the grass. I sat cross-legged with my back against the thick trunk and listened to the sounds of outside. Sometimes, when you closed your eyes and listened hard, you could hear a whole concert. Wind. Leaves rustling. A neighbor's trampoline squeaking. Kids laughing. A dog barking. Parents calling. Insects humming. Birds chirping.

Birds chirping!

I opened my eyes. Shel Silverstein sat in the tree right above me. He was still alone, even though I could have sworn I'd heard more than one bird.

"Hi!" I said, waving at him.

His flapping wings were a blur. I wished I had a slow-motion camera so I could see how they worked up close. He flew skyward, then swooped down and landed in front of me. He hopped across the grass toward me. When he chirped, it sounded like he was saying, *Hello, friend.*

I wasn't very good at whistling, but I gave it a shot. My whistle sounded kind of sandpapery.

He cocked his head to the side and chirped again, six short notes. His little song reminded me of all the robins singing in the mornings outside my window. So I tried to be like them, his family, his friends, and I sang the notes right back to him.

La-la, la-la, la-la.

We went back and forth like that for a while, as if we were having a conversation. Or a voice lesson. Sometimes Javier sang back and forth with me in the same way.

Shel Silverstein rotated his head to the side, jammed his beak into the grass, and plucked out a worm. Yuck!

He hopped away from me to devour his worm in private. As if he had to worry about me trying to take a bite. No thank you!

I pressed play on my voice recorder.

"Remember to breathe with your diaphragm, my friend," I said along with Javier's recorded lesson. Then I began to sing.

Shel Silverstein looked at me. He hopped over. Then he started singing along! I kept singing, and Shel Silverstein kept chirping. I couldn't decide if he was adding harmony or a backbeat, but whatever it was, it was a super fun duet.

Suddenly, Shel Silverstein screeched and darted away. He flew up, zooming high in the sky, before changing course and zipping down again. He landed on top of a tall bush at the back of our yard.

I jumped up and ran to him. "What happened? Are you okay?"

Our neighbor's calico cat was slinking under the bushes on the other side of our yard. She must have spooked him.

"That's just Clementine," I said to Shel Silverstein. "She won't hurt you. She lives a few houses down. She's a good cat."

But I wondered if that was true. Even good cats would attack birds. It was in their nature.

Shel Silverstein chirped in a higher octave than I'd heard him use before. His tiny legs shook. Poor little robin. He was terrified.

"Don't worry, nobody will hurt you while I'm around. I'll protect you from Clementine. I'll protect you from everything."

I reached out slowly to try to pet him. I wanted to smooth his feathers, help him calm down. But before I could make contact, he flew away.

&

Back inside the house, I went online and researched robins. I wanted to know what they did in the winter in northern Illinois. I found out that some robins did stay here all year. They needed four things to survive: food, water, shelter, and a flock.

I could help Shel Silverstein with food by making sure the feeder was always full. I could add extra raisins and cut-up apples for him. He wouldn't be able to find worms and insects anymore once the ground froze, so I'd have to be sure he had enough to eat.

The only way to make sure he'd have water that didn't freeze would be to buy a heated birdbath. I looked at them online, but they cost hundreds of dollars. Mom and Dad would most likely say no to that.

But I could build a birdhouse to provide shelter. They sold kits online, and they weren't too expensive.

I decided to ask for the birdhouse kit first and save my

request for the birdbath for later. Maybe on a perfect day when Sophie was behaving well, and no bills came to the house, and everyone had noticed how responsible I was about caring for Shel Silverstein.

The flock, however, was a problem. According to my research, a flock helped birds find food, water, and nesting places while steering them clear of predators. Somehow, I would have to persuade Shel Silverstein to make new friends.

I clicked off, drawn to the kitchen by the aroma of Winnie-the-Pooh Chicken. This was one of Dad's specialties, chicken in a honey sauce that was Sophie's and my favorite dish. Dad had made rice, carrots, and green beans too. Everything tasted delicious with Dad's sauce on it.

When we sat down to eat, I made lots of yummy sounds while I ate, which I knew made him happy. Then I said, "You know that family of robins who've been coming to our bird feeder? Well, I think they all flew south except for one who's still there. And he's going to need shelter for the winter. So I found a birdhouse kit online that's not too expensive, and I was wondering if maybe I could get it as an early Hanukkah present."

Dad looked at Mom.

Mom said, "We'll think about it, sweetie."

I knew what that meant: We want to say no but we don't want to disappoint you, so we'll say we'll think about it, but the truth is we hope you'll forget all about it.

I was not going to forget about it!

"Okay, but the robin is so little and cute. And I've even given him a name. Shel Silverstein."

Mom and Dad smiled at that.

"You have to see his sweet little face. Pleeease?"

"Ohhh," said Sophie. "Come on, guys. You let us make the bird feeder, which brought all the robins here. It doesn't seem fair to not take care of them in the winter."

I nodded and smiled at my sister. "Exactly!" I said.

Dad shrugged. "The girls do have a point," he said to Mom.

She said, "Okay, I'll look at it after dinner."

Yes!

Then Mom asked me what I'd decided about voice lessons versus hip-hop.

"Hip-hop it is!"

"What about Javier?" Sophie asked, a chicken drumstick halfway to her mouth.

"What about him?" I was starting to believe Sophie was the one with the crush on Javier, even though she only caught glimpses of him when Dad dropped me off or picked me up.

"I thought you loved him."

"I do. As. A. Teacher. If you love him so much, maybe you should take voice lessons."

Sophie's eyes lit up as she considered the idea, and I immediately wished I hadn't suggested it.

"Hold on a sec," Mom said. "Cass, are you sure that's what you want?"

I wasn't a hundred percent sure, but I nodded. What I wanted was to take both.

"Well, I have to say I'm surprised." Mom helped herself to more carrots and green beans. "And a little disappointed too. I love listening to you sing. You have a real gift. I hope you'll keep it up."

"Oh, I will. You don't have to worry about that." The thought of not singing was like the thought of not breathing or not thinking. Impossible. I took a bite of chicken.

"All right, so tomorrow will be your last voice lesson."

I shook my head. "Wait, no, hip-hop starts tomorrow. I can't go to voice."

Mom said, "I'm not canceling your lesson on such short notice. Besides, you should give Javier a proper goodbye. That's more respectful."

"But I can't miss the first day of hip-hop. I'll be behind."

"Sorry, Sunshine. You'll catch up."

Rats! It was one thing to think about quitting voice, but it was a whole different thing to think about having to tell Javier in person. "What if I were sick tomorrow? Then you'd cancel my voice lesson at the last minute."

"But you're not sick."

"Anyway," Dad said, "if you were sick, you wouldn't go to hip-hop either."

Ugh. Parents could be so frustrating sometimes.

"Can I quit therapy and take voice?" Sophie asked.

"No!" Mom and Dad both said at once.

Then, before Sophie could get upset, Mom said, "Who's ready for dessert?"

Distract and conquer. A common but useful strategy in our house.

Chapter Nine

The next day when I woke up Sophie, she said, "Happy favorite day of the week, Cass! Or is Wednesday not your favorite anymore because you have to say goodbye to Javier?"

"You know how it will be my favorite?" I asked. "If we get to school before first bell."

"Okay, okay, I'm moving," she said.

But she was curled in a ball under her blanket on the floor. Not moving at all.

"I'm going downstairs," I said.

"I'm moving, look." She shook her arms back and forth.

"Move your whole body," I said as I left her bedroom.

Shel Silverstein was alone in the tree again this morning. His bird feeder had plenty of seeds, but I wanted to bring him more fruit.

I made waffles and ate them so fast, Mom told me to slow down or I'd choke.

Sophie hadn't yet made it to the kitchen by the time I left for the tree with raisins and an apple cut in pieces. After I put it all in the feeder, Shel Silverstein chirped happily and dug in.

"Guess what?" I said to him. "I'm going to build you a birdhouse! Mom and Dad said yes to my early Hanukkah present request. So you can be safe in our yard when I'm not around. We'll put the birdhouse up high in the tree, right outside my window. We'll practically be roommates. Doesn't that sound good?"

Shel Silverstein cocked his head, then twitched his feathers. I took that to mean yes.

"But you need to make friends with some other birds while

I'm at school today. Just say hello. Maybe show them our feeder, or share a worm with them. Okay?"

Shel Silverstein didn't answer, as usual. This time I got the feeling he was ignoring me, the way Sophie ignored Mom sometimes when it was time to get in the shower or clean her room.

"Everyone needs a flock, Shel Silverstein."

I picked up a raisin and held it out to him. He plucked it right from my fingers.

❧

At recess, Lucy London said, "Okay, everybody, here's what you should wear to hip-hop today if you don't want to look like beginners. Leggings, any color. A cute tank top or T-shirt. And sneakers. Black and white striped are the best, like these." She kicked out her foot for us to see her black Adidas with white stripes.

I wondered why it would be so bad to look like beginners since that's exactly what we were, but I didn't say that out loud.

Holly said, "More dance talk? I'm outta here." She jumped down from the dome and went to play basketball with the boys.

Shayna left, too, saying she had to get something from the library.

I felt bad they were leaving, but that was their choice. Nobody had made them. I looked down at my lime-green Converse sneakers. Mom would never buy me new shoes, not until I grew out of the ones I had.

Dani had on pink Converse. "What about these?" she asked.

"Oh, those are cool too," Lucy said.

Phew!

I kicked my foot out to touch shoes with Dani, and we smiled at each other.

Lucy asked Evie if she was coming to hip-hop. When Evie said she was, she finally got her high five. I told Lucy my parents were making me go to one last voice lesson but that I'd be at hip-hop next week.

"Well...." Lucy said, and she seemed sort of mad. "As long as you don't skip any other classes, I guess that's okay."

Dani said, "We can show you what you miss."

"Thanks!" I said. "Maybe we can even have a dance club at recess."

"That's a fun idea," Dani said.

"I guess," said Lucy.

☙

I practiced what I would say to Javier all day, and I walked in the studio ready to say it: Javier, I'm really sorry, but I have to stop taking voice lessons because my parents can't afford it anymore, even with the scholarship.

It was sort of true. They couldn't afford for me to take singing *and* dance. I didn't have to tell him the whole truth. That would just hurt his feelings. I was hoping Javier would react the same way Dani did when Dad mentioned money. I was hoping he'd be embarrassed for me and want to change the subject. Then we'd finish my lesson and say goodbye. And next week I'd go to hip-hop.

But when I walked into the practice room, I got that happy feeling I got every time I saw Javier. He was wearing jeans and a flannel shirt. His wavy hair touched the middle of his collar. He was sitting on a stool with his guitar slung around his neck. He smiled and said hello as if seeing me walk in was the highlight of his week, not the other way around. I wondered if he made all his students feel like that.

All that happiness made it hard for me to say the words I'd planned to say.

I looked around at the album covers and band posters, and I thought about how *those musicians made music about true things*. Things that were so true that I felt it in the pit of my stomach. Javier always said that anyone could sing a song, but real artists sing something true.

That's what I wanted to do.

So I said, "Javier, I'm really sorry, but today is going to be my last lesson because I'm going to take hip-hop instead."

He opened his eyes wide. "Heep-hop, really?"

"Yes, I'm going to be a triple threat."

"What do you mean, triple threat?"

"Someone who can sing, dance, and act. That's how you get to be a star."

"Oh, so you want to be a star?"

"Yes." I felt a little silly saying that out loud to Javier, like I was saying, Look how great I am.

But he smiled and said, "I think you can be anything you want to be, my friend."

A tiny ball of light pulsed inside me.

"But this triple threat idea," he said, "that's for musicals, right? That's what you want? Like starring on Broadway. *Annie*? Or *Matilda*? *The Little Mermaid*?"

"I guess so."

He got up from his stool. Took his guitar off and sat at the piano. "So why are we singing folk and rock music?"

I shrugged. I didn't know I'd had a choice. Besides, I loved the songs we worked on together.

He started playing pieces of show tunes. "It's a Hard Knock Life," "Popular," "Do Re Mi."

I couldn't help but laugh. I liked those songs, but they were just so different from what I normally sang with him. That music seemed wrong surrounded by all his rock and folk album covers.

"Okay, so maybe not a Broadway star," I said.

"Tell me, Cassidy, why do you really want to take heep-hop?"

"Well, all my friends are taking it."

He didn't say anything, and it made me feel like I had to keep talking. Like I had to give him a better reason.

"And...I thought it would be fun."

More silence. Just a warm smile. I could picture him thinking, *Sing something true*, even though he didn't say it.

"And...well, I don't want to be left out."

Javier nodded, satisfied. But I had heard myself, and I realized how dumb I sounded. How totally uncool.

He said, "I see. Well, my friend, I will miss you. You are one of my favorite students. And we were just getting started together. But okay, you can become a triple threat with your friends." He went back to his guitar and pulled out some sheet music.

I had disappointed him. And myself. I wanted to shout, *April Fool's!* But it was October. I wanted to erase all the words I'd said. To him. To Mom and Dad. To Lucy London. It would feel terrible to be left out of hip-hop, but it would feel even worse to quit voice. I was a singer.

"So we are working on 'Summer Sky,' right?" he said. "Come, stand up straight."

He strummed the first chord.

"Wait," I said, my whole body buzzing. I didn't know what it was—fear, a little. And confidence, maybe. "You know what? I think my brain was confused, and actually I'm not quitting."

Javier put his hand to his chest. "No?"

"No," I said.

"Oh. But what about your friends?"

"I think, maybe, it will be okay." I hoped saying that would make it real.

Javier's happy eyes danced. He patted me on the head and ruffled my hair.

I turned on the recorder and sang "Summer Sky" with all my heart.

I didn't think about Lucy London and what might happen on Thursday. Not until the lesson was over.

Chapter Ten

The next morning I didn't even try to get to school early. I didn't want to tell Lucy and Dani I wasn't taking hip-hop, not until I absolutely had to. Every time I thought about what they might say, I came up blank. I wished I didn't like singing as much as I did. I wished Mom and Dad were rich so I could take every after-school activity I wanted. I wished that Lucy London had never moved to my town.

It was going to be a poop-emoji day for sure.

Instead of playing on the blacktop before first bell, I had to listen to Sophie whining again about wanting to be self-reliant in the morning but needing to eat eggs. The only good part of my morning was Shel Silverstein. I fed him a whole handful of raisins right out of my palm. But he was still alone. Those blue jays across the street weren't any closer to becoming his flock.

We got to school right before second bell, as usual. In PE, Mr. Davis timed us individually running the fifty-yard dash. While we waited our turns, I watched as Lucy, Dani, and the other girls danced at the side of the gym. Holly and Shayna stood with the boys, talking about boy stuff probably. I didn't want to join them. I wanted to be part of the dancing group. Even if I couldn't take hip-hop, I could still be in the dance club at recess. Actually, that was perfect. I could do both activities! Dance club at recess. Voice lessons on Wednesdays. Maybe I could even have a sleepover at Lucy's and get a mini-lesson with Sharon.

I walked over to the dancing girls. "You guys look awesome!" I said.

They all said thanks. They all said how much fun it was. They all said how cool Sharon was.

I got it.

"How did your last voice lesson go?" Dani asked.

"Well, actually…"

Lucy stopped dancing. "What happened?"

I took a deep breath. "So…I decided to stick with voice after all, but since we're gonna do dance club at recess I can do hip-hop then. So it's not really such a big deal."

Dani bit her lower lip. She looked upset.

Lucy made a face and said, "Um, I think it actually *is* a big deal."

"Wait. Why?"

"Dance club is for people taking hip-hop. Only. Otherwise, it would be too…basic."

"Basic?"

"You know, like for beginners. Slow. Boooorrring."

Everyone laughed at the way she said boring. Well, not Dani, but everyone else did.

"I know what basic means," I said. "But I'm a quick learner. It wouldn't have to be basic at all."

"Okay," Lucy said. "Let's see you dance. Here's the first sequence. It goes like this. Kick ball change step slide and hop. And left ball change slide hop and stomp." Her arms and legs moved as if there was a great beat playing that only she could hear, and she smiled like she was on stage.

Here's what I thought would happen next: I'd do it just like Lucy. I'd hip-hop like a pro, and Lucy and everyone would say things like, "Wow, you're really good!" And, "You don't even need to come to class! You're a natural triple threat!"

Here's what actually happened: My arms went one direction and my legs went another and I forgot the order of the steps and basically, I made a giant fool of myself.

Lucy laughed. "You really have to take the class to get it." Then she turned her back on me.

Dani said gently, "It's harder than it looks, Cass."

61

Maybe she was trying to comfort me, but I didn't feel comforted.

I said to her, "Just show me again."

Dani said, "It goes—"

Lucy put her hand up to stop her, and Dani took a step back. Then Lucy swung her ponytail while she spoke to the other girls, ignoring me. "Cassidy thinks she can do everything. But I guess she's not so perfect after all."

My heart pumped angry-angry-angry, and I yelled, "I never said I was perfect! You're the one who thinks she's so great!"

I was so loud that even the boys looked at me.

Dani's eyes went wide in surprise but she didn't come to my defense. Everyone else stared at me, too, but nobody said anything. I had the feeling I'd crossed some invisible line. Sweet, good Cassidy on one side, and out of control, unlikeable Cassidy on the other.

Was this what it felt like for Sophie every day?

One of the overhead lights flickered and buzzed. Mr. Davis blew his whistle and the boys went back to cheering for whomever was running.

Lucy said to the other girls, "Moving on, it goes out and in and turn and stomp. Ready?"

She was ignoring me, which somehow felt worse than if she had yelled back. The other girls followed along, doing the dance. Even Dani. Maybe she was embarrassed for me. Or mad at me. Maybe everyone was glad Lucy was ignoring me, so they could ignore me too.

I stood there, my hands in fists at my side. If I were Sophie, this is when I'd really lose it. Maybe I'd hit Lucy. Or kick her. Or even bite her. Maybe I'd go to Mr. Davis and complain that they were leaving me out.

But I wasn't Sophie. I was me. Cassidy Sunshine. So I stood there, doing nothing, feeling mad and alone and confused. I tucked all those feelings inside my junk drawer.

"Cassidy Carlson," Mr. Davis called. "You're on deck."

As I walked over to the starting line, none of my friends even looked in my direction. Only Eli Fleishman, over by the boys, yelled, "Go, Cassidy!" The girls weren't going to cheer me on. Maybe they weren't my friends after all. In fourth grade, the girls in my class were all friends. But in fifth grade, we seemed to be in some sort of competition.

And Lucy London was the prize.

I wanted to hate Lucy for changing everything, but I didn't. I remembered the first day of school, when she was new, and Mrs. Kwon asked her to introduce herself. She stood in front of the class, and with a clear, confident voice, she told us how she'd moved from New York City and that she had a sister named Grace and a cat named Mr. McCutie and that she loved dance and soccer. Then she said, "I can't wait to get to know you all and do so many fun things together." She was like a Miss America contestant.

There was something about Lucy London. She seemed older than us, and wiser, like she knew stuff we didn't. Maybe she could be a little harsh, but that was only because she was from somewhere else and more...I don't know...sophisticated than the rest of us. So, no, I didn't hate Lucy.

What I hated was that she didn't like me.

I felt so many emotions rise up inside me, like when you mix too many watercolor paints together and all you get is muddy brown.

Mr. Davis held up his stopwatch and said, "Ready?"

I nodded even though I wasn't ready at all.

"Get set."

He blew his whistle, and I ran.

❧

Sophie kicked a rock as we walked home from school while she told me about her day. But I wasn't listening. Recess had been a disaster because dance club was a hit. Even some of the boys came over and watched. By the end of recess, a couple of them had joined in and said they were going to ask their parents if they could take the hip-hop class, too. The boys!

I'd spent recess walking around the playground, pretending I was looking for someone. I felt terrible for yelling at Lucy. I couldn't believe I'd done that. But I also couldn't believe everyone was ignoring me. Even Dani. She barely spoke to me at lunch. She was just sort of polite. Best friends being polite to each other? That was more awkward than anything.

Shel Silverstein was around at recess, and I wanted to hang out with him. But I kept thinking about what Lucy London would say if she saw me spending recess with a bird, so I kept my distance.

Meanwhile, I couldn't take my eyes off dance club. Dani and Lucy were both great dancers. It was clear they were the leaders. I'd seen Dani dance just for fun, but this was something entirely different. Every move had an energy and power that made you want to see more. She was amazing.

I was happy for her. But a mean part of me was also jealous. And sad.

Dani was probably going to have another sleepover with Lucy. Maybe at Dani's house this time. And she wouldn't invite me because Lucy wouldn't want me there. Maggie would bring Lucy her stuffed elephant to say hello. Lucy would help herself to jelly beans. And they would make up a hip-hop dance together.

Sophie kept blabbing away to me, not noticing I wasn't paying attention. I wished she would just be quiet.

When we were almost home, Trey and Eli Fleishman caught up to us. "Wanna ride bikes?" Eli asked me.

"No, thank you." I adjusted my backpack.

"Okay, what about a video game?"

"No, thank you." I read the names on the tombstones at the fake cemetery in front of our neighbor's house.

"We could make Halloween decorations. My mom bought this totally gross blood and spider web stuff."

"No, thank you."

"Want to—"

Trey elbowed Eli to get him to stop.

I waved goodbye as we went up the walkway to our house.

"See you tomorrow!" Eli called after me.

"No, thank you!" Sophie called back, and I have to admit, I laughed.

Chapter Eleven

After we had a snack, Sophie said, "Let's have a cooking lesson. Fried eggs, anyone?"

"You're very persistent," Dad said. "Okay, this is a good time for all of us. And the master chef is ready. I'll teach both of you how to make eggs." He leaned toward us and said in a funny teachery voice, "The first thing you have to learn is how to crack open an egg."

Sophie pumped her fist and said, "Yes!" She opened the fridge and took the egg carton out.

I had a moment of hesitation. Shel Silverstein came from an egg. But it wasn't like these were robin eggs. And I didn't want to be a vegan anyway. So I decided it was okay to learn to make fried eggs. It would be good, actually, because I could use the stove and everything. Cooking eggs was a very advanced breakfast-making skill.

Dad put three bowls on the kitchen table, one for each of us. "Now this takes some practice. The goal is eggs in the bowl but no shells in the bowl. Right?"

"Right," Sophie and I said.

Dad opened the carton. There was one egg left. Uh-oh.

"Hmmm," Dad said. "It looks like I need to go to the grocery store."

"Daaaad!" Sophie said.

"Sorry," Dad said. "You can practice with this one if you want."

"Yeah," I said. "I don't mind."

Dad handed Sophie the egg.

She held it carefully in both hands. "What do I do?"

Dad said, "Gently but firmly tap it against the edge of the bowl."

Sophie shifted the egg into her right hand. She took a breath.

Tap, tap, tap.

"A little firmer than that," Dad said.

Tap, tap, tap.

We were going to be here all day.

"Honey, you have to use some force. You can do it."

Tap, tap, smash!

The egg cracked open and spilled all over the bowl, the table, and Sophie's hand. I was amazed one little egg could spread so far.

"Ew! Ew! Ew! It's touching me!" Sophie shook her hand, flinging trails of egg goo. A glob landed on my cheek.

Even though Sophie was freaking out, and laughter was not likely to help the situation, I couldn't stop myself. I giggled.

Sophie's face went from horrified and about to cry, to surprise, to amusement and glee. Then she laughed, in that loud, barky way that sometimes meant she was going to get dysregulated.

Dad dampened a paper towel and started cleaning up. "No problem, no problem," he said. "Eggs are on my shopping list, and we can try again this weekend."

"You'd better buy a lot of eggs," I said.

"Yeah," Sophie agreed. She was at the sink, scrubbing her hands.

"I will," Dad said. "Now why don't you girls go outside and play?"

Fresh air and running around would help Sophie forget about the broken egg. We grabbed rakes from the side of the house. Shel Silverstein was there, sitting on his bird feeder. He followed us into the backyard and hung out while we raked all the leaves into a giant pile. When the pile was almost as tall as me, Sophie and I took turns running at it. We started from a corner of the yard, dashed up, then leapt into the leaves, each time landing with a satisfying crunch.

We ran and jumped again and again, until the pile was squashed and leaves were scattered across the yard. Shel Silverstein made happy sounds as he flew around the backyard and hopped in the grass.

Running and jumping and playing with Sophie left no room for my friendship worries. It was just my sister and me.

We lay back on the leaves, breathing hard, and looked up at the sky. Shel Silverstein flew in a circle above us. I got the feeling we were filling him with joy.

"Look at that bird!" Sophie said. "I wish I could fly. Don't you?"

"Uh-huh. That's the robin I was telling you about. Shel Silverstein. The one I'm making a birdhouse for."

"Can I help you make the birdhouse? Can I help take care of him?"

"Sure!"

"Leaf angels!" Sophie said, and she swung her arms and legs back and forth as if we were making snow angels.

I copied her, and even though the air was cool, I felt warm from my head to my toes.

> ৶

Later that afternoon, while Dad was cutting vegetables at the kitchen counter, I sat at the table with Sophie. We were supposed to be doing our homework. Sophie's math book was open in front of her, but she was drawing rows of kittens in her spiral notebook. I had a list of vocabulary words from our reading group that I had to write sentences for, but my mind was on my own problems.

Analyze: to examine carefully, study closely.

I am trying to analyze what is going on with my friends.

I thought about Mrs. Kwon reading that sentence and

68

decided it would be smarter to keep my friendship trouble out of it, so I erased and rewrote the sentence.

Curtis is trying to analyze what is going on with his friends.

Better.

Apparent: obvious, easy to see.

It is not very apparent why Leon would be so mean to Curtis.

Awkward: lacking grace or skill in manner, movement, or performance.

Curtis is awkward at basketball, and now that has made him feel awkward with his friends.

I wondered if Mrs. Kwon would give me extra credit for using awkward twice.

Burrow: a hole in the ground made by an animal for shelter.

Today in PE, Curtis wished he could go into a burrow and hide from everyone.

Coax: to persuade or urge in a gentle way.

Curtis will have to find a way to coax Leon to like him.

I stopped right there, even though I still had more sentences to write. If only I could coax Lucy London to like me.

The key to making friends was finding things you had in common. That's what Mom always told Sophie, anyway. She was probably right. It sounded smart.

So what did Lucy and I have in common? We were both good students. That was something. But maybe it wasn't such a good thing to have in common because Lucy wanted to be the *best* student. Lucy liked dancing, and I liked singing, so we both liked to perform. Also, Lucy liked coming up with fun recess ideas, and I liked coming up with fun recess ideas. Before Lucy joined our class, I invented some of the best recess activities ever. One week we did a version of *America's Got Talent.* And a lot of times we did make-believe, only more advanced. We'd take one of our favorite books or TV shows and act it out. All my ideas. Dance club was actually my idea too.

Leave it to me to come up with a recess plan that ended up getting me excluded!

Disaster: something that causes great damage or harm.

Curtis knew that having no friends would be a total disaster.

I sat up straighter and thought some more. And then a lightning bolt hit me in the form of the best recess idea ever. We could do a musical. And I would write it!

A musical would be seriously advanced make-believe. There would be singing *and* dancing. It could include hip-hop. That would make Lucy happy. And Dani. And everyone!

I stood up and moved to the center of the kitchen. Then I attempted the dance sequence Lucy had done at gym class. I was just as awkward as before, but this time I added a spin and a kick and a curtsy. I felt myself smile as I flung my hair off my shoulder. I might not have a shiny, swingy ponytail, but my hair was pretty in its own way.

Sophie said, "Wow!" Then she stood up and started dancing. Her moves were wild and jerky. She said, "Oh yeah, oh yeah, check me out!"

Dad said, "Whoa, girls. Settle down." He gave me a look like I should have known better than to rile Sophie up like that. "Back to your homework, please."

"It was just a dance break, Dad," Sophie said. "I can focus. Watch." She sat down and looked intensely at her math homework. She scribbled a bunch of nonsense numbers in her notebook all around the kittens she'd drawn.

"Sophie," Dad said in a warning voice.

"Okay, okay." She took a deep breath.

"Sorry," I said. I took out a fresh piece of paper and settled down to write my play. First things first—a title. Hmmm...I looked around.

Sophie. Kittens. Math homework. Dad. Vegetables. Vocabulary words. I twirled my pencil between my fingers. Titles were hard.

Just then, Mom came home. She slipped off her shoes and dropped her purse, keys, and phone on the counter. "Ugh, what a day. I hate preparing budgets." She picked a slice of red bell pepper off the cutting board and popped it into her mouth.

"Hawaiian stir fry for dinner," Dad said.

"Hawaii." Mom had a dreamy look on her face. "Let's all escape to Hawaii."

"Really?" Sophie said.

Mom sighed. "I wish."

Sophie said, "Hawaii, Hawaii, Hawaii, Hawaii."

It was Mom's turn to take a deep breath. "How are my girls? How was school?"

"Good," we both said.

I wasn't about to tell her the truth.

"Good," Mom said. "Good, good, good." Then she walked right out of the kitchen and into the family room.

Dad whispered in my ear, "Cass, go give Mom a little sunshine, will you?"

Sophie was flipping through the pages of her math book as Dad sat down next to her. He asked her which page she was supposed to be on.

I hopped up and followed Mom into the family room. She was lying on the sofa, one arm draped over her forehead. I snuggled in next to her.

"Hi, sweetie," she said.

"Hi, Mama."

I tickled her arm the way I knew she liked. Then I touched all the freckles on her face. "I love you, Mama."

She squeezed me tight, kissed me on my nose, and smiled. "Cassidy Sunshine, what would I do without you?"

❧

After dinner I went to my room and worked on the musical. I came up with a title: *The Funky Kittens vs. The Volcano.* The

71

story would take place in Hawaii and it would be narrated by a talking bird. A volcano is about to erupt, and the only way to stop it is if the volcano is entertained. So all kinds of people, like magicians and singers and comedians or whatever, try to entertain the volcano. But it's not until the Funky Kittens, a group of hip-hop dancing girls, do an incredible dance that the volcano cools off and there is no eruption and everyone is safe.

I made a list of all the characters. I even wrote out some dialogue and the beginning of a song. My musical needed a lot of work, but it was a good start.

Sometimes, when things seem terrible, you just have to do something new, anything, to begin to feel better.

Chapter Twelve

I made another list.

THINGS TO DO AT RECESS WHEN YOUR FRIENDS EXCLUDE YOU FROM THE DANCE CLUB YOU INVENTED:

1. *Walk around, pretending to look for somebody.*
2. *Go to the library.*
3. *Join the other kids who don't have friends.*
4. *Talk to the recess monitor.*
5. *Trade Pokémon cards with your sister and her friends.*
6. *Wave hello to a special bird without anyone seeing, and watch him soar.*

On Friday, I tried everything on the list except trading Pokémon cards. I liked playing with Sophie at home, but I didn't like Pokémon cards, and I didn't want to hang out with my sister at recess. School was school, and home was home. They were different, and I wanted to keep it that way.

Recess seemed to last twice as long as normal.

The worst part of being excluded was Dani. She was acting different. Like she was mad at me. Or like I didn't matter. Like Lucy was everything.

I had to hurry up and finish my musical so that I could get back in with my friends. The musical would make everything right again.

❧

On Saturday morning, Dad called upstairs to say the cooking lesson was starting.

When I walked in the kitchen, Mom was sitting at the table drinking coffee, but Sophie wasn't there.

"Soph!" Dad yelled up the stairs.

"No, thank you," she called down.

Mom, Dad, and I looked at each other. Then Dad trudged upstairs.

"Can I smell your coffee?" I asked.

Mom slid the steaming mug across the table until it sat in front of me. I wrapped my hands around the warm cup and took a big sniff. I loved the way coffee smelled but hated the way it tasted. Sort of the opposite of broccoli. I loved the way broccoli tasted, but every time Dad cooked it, the kitchen got all stinky. Weird.

Dad came downstairs with Sophie, but she didn't look eager to start a cooking lesson. She looked scared.

"What's wrong?" I asked.

"I'm afraid of eggs now," Sophie said.

Dad jumped in. "But we're not going to let that stop us because I bought four cartons of eggs. Sophie is going to conquer her fear." He pumped his fist in the air, like he was a soccer coach or something.

"I don't think so," Sophie said. "And now I'm conflicted because I really, really, really want to be self-reliant in the mornings. But." She shuddered. "Egg goo."

"First things first, we'll wash hands," Dad said, ignoring Sophie's protests.

I went to the sink. Sophie stayed slouched at the table. I said, "Come on, Soph. You're not afraid of washing your hands."

"Fine. But I'm not touching the eggs."

"One step at a time," Dad said.

After our hands were clean, Dad set us up at the table with bowls and eggs. Then he demonstrated the proper egg-cracking technique. After breaking a few neatly into his bowl, he showed off, cracking an egg open with one hand. "That's for master chefs only," he said.

Mom raised her eyebrows and smirked. Dad wasn't really a

74

master chef, but he did watch a lot of cooking shows on TV.

It was our turn to try.

"I can't touch an egg," Sophie said. "I can't!"

"Sure you can," Dad said. "If anything gets on you again, you can wash it off. No big deal."

"I caaaan't!"

Mom said, "I have an idea." She brought out a pair of rubber gloves from under the sink.

Sophie put on the gloves, picked up an egg, and stared at it.

I picked up an egg and tap, tap, tapped it just the way Dad had shown us. It cracked right down the middle. I pulled the sides apart, and the egg plopped into the bowl. "Wow!" I said. Maybe I was meant to be a master chef someday!

"Nice job!" Dad said.

"Well done!" Mom said.

Sophie burst into tears. "Everything is so easy for Cass!" Her sad face turned angry, scrunchy and red. "It's not fair!"

All the air rushed out of me. "That's not true!"

"Name one thing!" she said. "One thing that's harder for you than me."

I stood there, speechless. I hated that Sophie could turn something that should have been fun, like cracking eggs, into something mean and yucky. Now there was another thing for me to feel guilty about.

Mom said, "That's enough, girls." Her nostrils flared. She turned to Dad. "It would have been smarter to do individual lessons."

Dad put his hands up in defeat. "Maybe you could have made that helpful suggestion beforehand."

Now everyone was mad. I ran out of the kitchen.

I went to my room and slammed the door. I made my deep-down secret wish.

Then I opened the window. Shel Silverstein was there, in his golden tree. He was preening his feathers. Maybe he was

75

lucky to be alone. He didn't have to worry about problems with the other birds. No birds around to make him feel clumsy or awkward. No birds to make him feel like his life was so much easier than theirs. No birds to make him feel guilty, or responsible, or anything.

"Why didn't you fly south with your family?" I asked him. "Was it a mistake or did you stay back on purpose?"

Shel Silverstein tilted his head to the side, listening.

Maybe he had stayed in the tree because he wanted to. Maybe he'd been stubborn, the way Sophie was sometimes, and he refused to go. And when they left, he was like, *Fine, I didn't want to go anyway.* But then he got sad and lonely when he realized they were really gone. That happened to Sophie once when she refused to go to the Wisconsin State Fair. I ended up going with Mom, and Dad and Sophie stayed home. She was sorry afterward.

I sighed.

The wind blew and the leaves rustled. A few leaves drifted down to the ground.

"Sometimes I imagine what it would be like to live in a different family," I told Shel Silverstein. "In Dani's family, specifically. But then I get scared that if I think like that too often, it might come true. Do you know what I mean?"

He chirped, and it sounded like he was saying, *Uh-huh, uh-huh, uh-huh.*

I stared at Shel Silverstein's missing piece in the circle above his eye. I wondered if I still had that book. I left the window to search my bookcase and found it on the bottom shelf.

I stretched out on my bed and read it. Then I read *The Giving Tree.* But I couldn't get Lucy London's voice out of my head. Maybe the tree had been foolish for giving everything away. But how else was the tree supposed to show her love for the boy?

After that, I read a bunch of my other picture books, old books I hadn't opened in years. When I was younger, Mom,

Dad, Sophie, and I used to all snuggle together in one bed, enjoying these stories. We would trade nights between Sophie's room and mine. Sophie always got to choose the last book we'd read before lights out. And I never minded.

I put the books away and worked on my musical. I didn't think about my friends. Or Sophie. Or SPD. Or fairness. Or eggs.

We ate a lot of eggs that weekend.

Chapter Thirteen

On Monday at recess, it was a re-do of Friday. Nothing had changed. Dani was still either ignoring me or being strangely polite. Everyone was still doing dance club without me. And I was still counting the minutes until recess ended.

But it was Monday. Which meant I was supposed to go to Dani's house after school. I wasn't sure if that was going to happen. She hadn't broken her plans with me, so maybe that meant we were still on.

At the end of the day, I walked over to Dani at her cubby. "Vampire scarecrow?"

"Oh," she said. Then she looked awkwardly at Lucy London. So she wanted to invite Lucy too.

That was fine with me. That was actually great because Lucy and I would get to know each other better. I could find out more things we had in common. "Lucy can come too," I said.

Dani said, "No…actually…I'm so sorry I didn't tell you sooner, but I'm taking another dance class on Mondays now."

"Oh," I said, trying to sound like my heart was still in one piece.

Lucy said, "Dani's really good. My mom said she could take the advanced class with me."

"That's great," I said. "I'm happy for you."

Dani touched my elbow. "I'm really sorry, Cass. Maybe we could do Halloween decorations a different day."

"No, it's fine," I said, ignoring the tug in my chest. I plastered a smile on my face. I wasn't about to lose it like I had in PE the other day. Just because Dani was taking an extra dance class didn't mean we weren't still best friends. Besides, I was writing

78

a musical that would bring us all together. "You know, I'm busy today anyway. I'm…working on a secret project."

Here's what I thought would happen next: Dani would ask me about the project, and I'd tell her about the musical, and she would love it, and so would Lucy, and everything would be right again.

Here's what actually happened: Dani said, "That's great!"

Then Lucy said, "We gotta go."

And off they went, Lucy's ponytail swinging.

❧

I lied to Dad after I came home from school. I told him Dani was sick, and that's why I couldn't go to her house.

The lie was like lemonade. Smooth and easy to swallow. It was Dad's reaction that left a bad taste in my mouth. He didn't doubt me for a second.

There was a part of me that wanted him to know the truth. Like if he knew I was lying, that meant I was somehow safer. Like my parents were really in charge. And maybe he could fix everything. Still, a bigger part of me didn't want him to know. After all, I was the one Mom and Dad didn't have to worry about. The one who cooperated, who did well in school and made friends easily. I was Cassidy Sunshine—that's who Mom and Dad needed me to be.

I didn't want to go to Sophie's therapy appointment. It would remind me of watching Dani make the friendship bracelet for Lucy London. So I said, "Dad, I think I'm old enough to stay home alone while you take Sophie to therapy."

"Hmmm…You sure, Sunshine?"

"Yeah, I'll be fine. I won't let any strangers in. And I won't burn down the house, I promise."

Dad laughed and ruffled my hair. "Okay, kiddo. This isn't your secret plan to throw a big party, is it? Did you turn into a rebellious teenager while I wasn't looking?"

"Very funny."

"Hold on!" Sophie said. "You're letting Cass stay home alone? I'm not allowed to stay home alone."

Dad said, "Because you would have a giant party. With boys. I know what you're all about!"

"Daaad!" Sophie whined, but she was laughing too. Neither of us would have a giant party, and Dad knew it.

He gave me a kiss on the forehead and left with Sophie before her mood could change.

I realized it was my first time being all alone in our house. It felt kind of weird but also kind of cool.

I walked from room to room. It was so quiet. I kept feeling like Sophie was just around the corner or Mom was in the kitchen or Dad was in his office. But there I was, alone in an empty house.

I wanted this, I reminded myself.

No. What I really wanted was to be at Dani's.

I turned on the radio in the kitchen. I sang along to P!nk, but for some reason I didn't get my bubbly feeling. I kept thinking about Dani.

And Lucy.

Dani and Lucy.

I wondered what their dance class was like. What were they doing exactly? It wasn't fair that I'd never been to Lucy's apartment or the dance studio. And why did Dani think it would be okay to take a dance class on *our* Mondays?

I looked at the clock on the microwave. Dad and Sophie wouldn't be home for another whole hour. An hour would give me plenty of time to ride my bike into town. I knew where Lucy lived from the time we played Bakiwang Says. Downtown, next to the fountain, over the studio. So I could go there. I could peek in the window. I could see what was happening at the studio and what all the excitement was about. It was a free country, after all.

I left a note for Dad, just in case he got home before I did, telling him I was riding my bike. I heard Dad's voice in my head, so I made sure to lock the house and close the garage. And I wore my helmet. I walked over to the side of the house and looked up into Shel Silverstein's tree. He was there, sitting on the branch outside my bedroom window.

"I'm going bike riding!" I called up to him. "Want to come?"

Shel Silverstein fluttered down to greet me.

He was even better than a dog. Because dogs don't fly.

While I rode my bike, Shel Silverstein flew alongside. I kept my eyes peeled for Clementine and any other potential dangers, but it was smooth sailing. I loved the way the cool wind rushed past my ears.

When I rode up next to the fountain, Shel Silverstein floated down to the shallow pool and settled there. He splashed around and pecked at the water. Other birds perched on the top of the fountain. Including blue jays! Maybe Shel Silverstein would finally make friends.

"Hi, jays!" I said, waving. Fortunately, nobody else was standing around the fountain, wondering about a girl talking to the birds.

Shel Silverstein looked up. The jays looked down. Then the jays swooped into the water, making a big splash.

Shel Silverstein hopped away to the other side of the fountain. The jays were bigger than him. And squawkier. But still. There they all were, in the fountain together. It was practically a pool party.

"Shel Silverstein, meet the blue jays. Blue jays, meet Shel Silverstein."

The birds all hopped and splashed and preened.

"You guys have a lot in common. You're all birds, of course. And you like fountains."

One of the jays flew up and zoomed around in a circle over

my head. Then, plop! Bird poop landed on the shoulder of my jean jacket. Gross!

"And, clearly, you all poop."

Getting pooped on by a bird was supposed to be good luck, so I wasn't too upset. Even though it was pretty disgusting.

I left the birds splashing around and went to look for Fusion Two. But first I needed a bathroom so I could clean off my jacket.

Restaurants and shops surrounded the fountain. There was a bookstore, a drugstore, a couple of clothing shops, a deli, a diner, and an Indian restaurant. But I didn't see a dance studio.

I left my bike out in front of the bookstore while I used their bathroom to clean up. Afterward, my shoulder had a huge wet spot, but that was better than blue-jay poop.

I walked around the downtown area again until I found a door next to the Indian restaurant that had a small sign on it. "Fusion Two, second floor."

I opened the door and walked up the narrow stairs, singing under my breath as I climbed.

It smelled like curry from the restaurant. As I got closer to the second floor, I heard hip-hop music.

Another door. On the other side, I could hear Sharon counting the beat and giving instructions. Feet stomped. Girls laughed. It sounded so fun.

I stood there, not sure what to do. I'd come all this way without really thinking it through. I'd imagined a storefront window, an easy view to see inside the studio. Not this. Not me, standing here, listening in, feeling more like an outsider than ever.

I could turn back, I thought. I probably should turn back.

Or I could knock.

Or just...open the door.

I opened the door.

There was no lobby. There was no reception area. I stepped right inside the dance studio.

A wood floor. A bar along one wall. Cubbies along another wall. And in front of me, reflecting me to all ten girls and Sharon, a fully mirrored wall.

Everyone stared at me. Sharon paused the music. "Hi! Can I help you?"

"Um..." My brain stopped. It just...stopped.

Dani said, "Cass?"

Lucy said, "What are you doing here?"

And then this came out of my mouth: "I was just passing by."

In the mirror, I saw it all so clearly. Me, wearing a jean jacket with a giant wet spot and a bike helmet I'd forgotten to take off. Dani and Lucy with the other dancers, everyone looking cool and strong and together.

I was the intruder.

And what had I said? That I was passing by? Oh no! How embarrassing!

"I mean, actually, I was picking up dinner for my family. At the Indian restaurant? Downstairs? So...I better go. See ya!"

I turned and fled.

I blinked back tears as I ran down the stairs. What had I done?

Before I could exit the building, I heard footsteps behind me. I glanced over my shoulder, afraid it was Sharon ready to scold me for intruding on the class.

But it was Dani.

Her hair was pulled back in a ponytail, but it wasn't neat and shiny like Lucy London's. The stray hairs sticking out gave me a weird sense of comfort.

"Cass," she said. "What are you doing?"

I shook my head and shrugged.

"I thought we were all three going to be best friends," she said.

"I thought so too."

"But why are you acting so weird? Why are you being so strange with Lucy? You keep making it too hard."

Here's what I wanted to say next: I don't mean to. But I'm worried Lucy London doesn't want to be friends with me. I'm worried she wants you all to herself. And I'm really worried you might want that too.

Here's what I actually said: "I'm not acting weird. I was going to pick up dinner, and I noticed the Fusion Two sign, so I came up to say hi. How's that weird?"

Today was a lying day, for sure.

Dani stared into my eyes. "You hate Indian food."

I looked at a spot on the wall behind her. "Maybe I used to. But things change, I guess."

"I guess they do," she said.

I had a feeling neither of us was talking about Indian food.

Chapter Fourteen

Dani came to school with her hair in a ponytail on Tuesday. And she was wearing black Adidas with white stripes.

While I wandered around at recess, I told myself they were just shoes. It didn't matter.

But I was not very convincing.

I wondered if in middle school I'd say to Dani, *Remember when we used to be best friends?* And neither of us would laugh because it wouldn't be funny.

Making friends had always been easy for me, but Dani was right. Everything I did around Lucy seemed wrong. I had to finish the musical. That wouldn't be wrong. That would be the rightest thing ever. So I went to the library to finish it.

I sat at one of the desks and went to work. Too bad I didn't know how to write music. I had melodies in my head, but all I could write were the lyrics. Maybe Javier could teach me.

When I got stuck figuring out what I could rhyme with "pizzazz," I asked the librarian for help. Ms. Codell showed me a great online rhyming dictionary, and soon I was lost in the internet of words. I loved all the rhymes and definitions. So many choices! Eventually, I found razzmatazz, which worked perfectly for the song for the Funky Kittens. The bell rang way too soon.

I walked back to the classroom, thinking about how writing the musical with the internet to help me had made it better and more fun. Maybe I didn't have to finish the whole thing before I shared it with Lucy and Dani. In fact, it might be better and more fun if we all worked on it together.

Yes! As I took my seat, I decided I would tell them about the musical the next day at recess. And we'd finish writing it together. And soon enough, we'd all be friends. Maybe even best.

❧

When Sophie and I got home from school, a package was sitting at the front door. The birdhouse kit!

We opened it up and inside were all the pieces, each one sanded smooth, plus six little pots of paint and a paintbrush.

"Can we build it now, Dad?" I asked.

Dad looked at the instructions. "Sure. But let's have a snack first."

I twirled in a circle.

"Dad, don't forget you have to help me with the…" Sophie whispered, "egg thingy."

I didn't know what she was talking about, but she'd been whispering to Dad about eggs ever since her therapy session.

Sophie and I ate cheese and crackers at the kitchen table, while Dad spread out newspaper and got a tube of wood glue from the garage.

Sophie said, "Remember, you said I could help."

I nodded. "I know. But we'll have to take turns because there's only one paintbrush."

"Okay, and you can go first because it was your idea, so that's fair."

Sophie definitely liked things to be fair. Painting the birdhouse with my sister might be a little messier and take a little longer, but I didn't mind.

After Dad helped us fit the pieces together, and after Sophie changed out of her new skort-turned-top so she wouldn't get paint on it, we took turns using the brush. We painted the front and back yellow, the roof green, the sides blue, and the base purple. Once that was done, we decorated the roof with white daisies, which didn't turn out so great. It was hard for both of us to do those. We painted a big red heart on the back, and we finished it off with a purple *SS*, for Shel Silverstein, above his front door.

❧

On Wednesday morning, I ran down to the kitchen and picked up the birdhouse. The paint had dried. "Isn't it so cute?" I asked Mom.

"It certainly is."

"Can we hang it now?"

"Oh, Sunshine, I don't think so. I'm not climbing a ladder dressed like this. Dad will help you hang it after school."

"I can do it myself. I climb up the ladder to fill the feeder all the time."

"But you'll want to make sure it's secure. Dad will help."

"Can I at least show Shel Silverstein?"

Mom laughed. "Okay, but eat your breakfast first. I made cheesy scrambled eggs, and they're hot."

Sophie walked into the kitchen. She was wearing purple leggings and a yellow top with a big daisy on it. She had a plastic flower tucked behind her ear, and she'd cut fringe in the bottom of her leggings that swished when she walked. "Oh, it looks so good," she said, admiring the birdhouse. "It's almost like we have a pet!"

"Yep!"

Shel Silverstein was even better than a pet. He was wild, and he'd chosen me.

Sophie and I sat at the table with the birdhouse between us like a centerpiece. We ate eggs and toast, and we watched out the window as Shel Silverstein hopped around in the grass searching for worms.

Sophie said, "Can you show me how to do the food for the feeder? I want to be able to do that too."

"It's not a big deal. I just scoop some out of the bag, and I add extra raisins and sometimes apples. Then I pour it in the feeder."

"Okay, I'll do that today. Will you watch me to make sure I do it right?"

"Sure."

After I cleared my place, I got the plastic bowl I used for scooping and gave it to Sophie.

"How much?" she asked, opening the pantry.

"It doesn't really matter."

"Is this good?" The bowl was only about a quarter of the way full.

"Maybe a little more."

When she added more seed to the bowl, she tipped the bag too much and the seed spilled out, scattering all over the pantry shelf. "Uh-oh!"

"It's fine," I said. "I'll clean it up."

"No, I can do it." She started sweeping the seeds with her hand into the bag, but they landed on the floor.

Mom said, "Soph, let Cass help you with that."

"No, I got it."

This was going to take all day. I looked outside to check on Shel Silverstein. He'd found a worm. He was tugging and tugging. Suddenly a movement in the corner of the yard caught my eye. Clementine, flicking her tail.

I dashed outside and yelled, "Watch out!"

Shel Silverstein flew up from the grass. Clementine leaped across the lawn, through our bushes, and into Eli's yard.

My heart was going a million miles an hour.

Shel Silverstein circled me. "Are you okay?" I asked him.

He landed on the grass near my feet and gave himself a shake. Then he started preening his feathers.

My legs felt like Jell-O. I sat down in the grass and wrapped my arms around my knees. He could have been killed! I had to get that birdhouse up today. And Shel Silverstein had to find a flock.

"Promise me you'll find a new flock today. Please," I begged him.

I reached out to touch him. I still hadn't been able to feel his feathers. We were about an inch apart when he hopped backwards, creating more space.

"Okay, fine," I said, pulling my hand back. "But listen. If it's not the jays, it has to be some other birds. Everyone needs a flock."

He tilted his head down. Then he looked up at me with his sad eyes. It seemed like he was saying, *Easy for you to say.*

I thought about Dani. She sort of flew south without me... if Lucy London were south. And it wasn't like I wanted to suddenly become best friends with Holly or Monique or Shayna or Evie, or really anyone else. I wanted to be best friends with Dani. Because Dani was my best friend.

"You still miss your family, don't you?"

Shel Silverstein chirped.

"I get it. But they'll be back in the spring, I know they will. And in the meantime, you have to do what it takes to get through the winter so they'll be able to find you when they return. Okay?"

I stared at his pointy little beak and those black eyes circled in white. The missing piece above his right eye.

I loved this little bird.

"Listen," I said. "Today I'm going to tell Lucy and Dani about my musical, and everything's going to be better after that. And you need to have a great day too. Okay? We'll both have smiley-face-emoji days. Maybe even smileys-with-hearts days."

I reached out to Shel Silverstein, like he could slap me five. He hopped close and gently pecked my hand.

Chapter Fifteen

At recess that day, I watched as everyone gathered for dance club. Again.

But today would be different. Today they'd hear about my musical, which they would love. How could they not? The hip-hop dancers would be the stars of the show. And we'd work on it together. Soon, we'd all be friends.

"Hey," I said, walking over to dance club. "I have an idea for something new we can do."

They all turned to look at me. My heart did a little flip-flop. I opened my mouth to say something, but nothing came out.

"What is it?" Lucy said.

"It's, um, a play. A, like, a musical."

They were all still listening, so I started talking faster. "There will be singing. And hip-hop. And it's about The Funky Kittens—a group of dancing girls."

Dani smiled. "Cool!"

I felt myself smile. "Yeah. And a volcano is going to erupt. See, they're in Hawaii. And the volcano needs to be entertained and the magician can't do it and the singer can't do it and the comedian can't do it and…"

"That sounds complicated," Lucy said, her ponytail swinging.

My heart skipped a beat.

"Yeah," everyone else agreed.

I looked at Dani. She bit her bottom lip. She glanced at Lucy and then the ground.

She wasn't coming to my rescue. I felt a huge lump in my throat, and all I could do was blink really fast to keep my eyes from doing anything stupid, like making tears.

"Besides, we'd have to write the whole thing," Lucy said. "That would take forever."

"But I've already written a lot of it," I said, in a voice I wished sounded stronger.

Dani was staring so hard at the ground, I thought she could burn a hole in the woodchips.

"And we'd need props and costumes and a stage. Not to mention rehearsals," Lucy said. "It's kind of a dumb idea. No offense."

"Yeah," everyone said. Except Dani. She was still studying the ground.

No offense? How could she call me dumb and say no offense?

Dani twisted the toe of her shoe into the woodchips. Then, finally, she looked at me. The expression on her face meant she was trying to tell me to drop the whole idea. To not cause a scene like I'd done in PE or at Fusion Two.

Here's what I wanted to do: pull Lucy London's ponytail right out of her head.

Here's what I actually did: I listened to Dani's face. I said, "Yeah, you're right. It's kind of complicated for recess."

Dani looked relieved, which made me mad. I wanted to walk away, but it felt like walking away would be like walking away forever. I tried to tell Dani that with my face. I sent her all the best-friend energy I could, saying, *Do something to help me!*

And she must have understood, because she said, "We don't have to do dance club every day, do we? I mean, I bet you have lots of good ideas from your old school, Lucy."

Lucy said, "Oh, I for sure do. And they're way easier than putting on a musical."

Ouch.

That stung. But I had to hand it to Dani. She knew just how to get Lucy to stop doing dance club and include me.

I was barely able to listen as Lucy described yet another recess

91

idea. It sounded like a combination of catch and concentration. Something about standing in a circle and throwing a ball and naming things in categories.

I was sure I'd hate the game. Because Lucy London was bossy, and the game was stupid, and everyone was mean. But I played because it wasn't dance club, and Dani had done this for me. She'd heard my best-friend silent communication, and she'd found a way to include me.

Maybe our friendship wasn't ending.

After a couple of rounds, I found myself having fun. Rats. It would be way easier to hate Lucy London if her ideas weren't so good.

I had to face the truth. Lucy was good at recess ideas, and I wasn't. My musical was too complicated. Another truth: Dani really liked Lucy. Maybe more than she liked me. Maybe Dani deserved a best friend like Lucy, someone who could dance and come up with fun things to do and didn't have a sister who would ruin sleepovers.

We were in the middle of a round with the category of cities when Sophie came over, waving her arms and calling, "Cass! Cass! Cass!"

The ball had just been passed to me, so I held it and said, "What?"

"I have some very exciting news to share with you." She bounced up and down, too happy to stand still. "You know how tonight's the sixth-grade fall assembly?"

"Yeah?"

"Well, Adam Greeley was absent today because he has strep throat, and he was supposed to have a speaking part so I asked Mrs. Diamond if I could have his part and guess what, guess what? She said I could. Isn't that great?"

Sophie was smiling so proudly.

I said, "That really is great, Soph!" And I meant it. Sophie didn't get many chances to shine.

Dani said, "That's exciting, Sophie."

Lucy said, "Cass, it's your turn. Come on."

So I threw the ball, but I forgot to name a city.

"You're out," Lucy said.

Shoot. I was.

I sat down in my spot, waiting for the next round to start. I watched Sophie bop around the playground. She was telling her exciting news to everyone who would listen.

At the fifth-grade fall assembly, when I got to sing that solo in front of all four fifth-grade classes and the parents and grandparents and brothers and sisters, I'd been so nervous about it beforehand that I hadn't been able to eat dinner, even though it was barbecued chicken and dill pickles, my favorite. If Sophie got nervous and didn't eat, there'd be trouble. Being hungry and nervous would definitely set off her broken thermometer. But she was happy at the moment. And maybe she wouldn't get nervous before the show. Maybe she'd eat dinner and feel calm and everything would be fine.

๛

After recess, Mrs. Kwon returned our vocab homework. Instead of seeing the usual *Great job!* written on my paper, I saw: *See me after the final bell, please.* ☺

It was hard to pay attention after that. I'd never been asked to see a teacher after school. It meant I was in trouble, but I didn't know what for. Then again, there was a smiley face. Maybe I wasn't in trouble. Maybe my sentences were so good Mrs. Kwon wanted to enter me into some sort of vocabulary bee.

At the end of the day, we all lined up for our fist bump, high five, or hug. I took my time packing my backpack so I'd be last in line. That way, nobody would realize I was staying after school.

When everyone else was gone, Mrs. Kwon said, "Cassidy, thanks for staying."

"You're welcome," I said, even though I didn't know I'd had a choice.

Mrs. Kwon sat down at one of the kid desks, her knees all bunched up high. She tapped the seat next to her and I sat there. "So listen," she said. "I read your vocabulary homework, and I was wondering if you wanted to talk. Is anything going on socially for you that you might need some help with?"

My heart started beating super fast. I felt like I'd been caught doing something wrong. I shook my head no.

"Because if there's a problem, you can talk to me." Mrs. Kwon smiled. Her face had a kind, patient expression.

I thought about telling her what was going on. But I didn't know how to even start to explain it. Plus, I didn't want to get Lucy in trouble for leaving me out of dance club. That would only make things worse. And what if Mrs. Kwon called my parents? They had enough to worry about with Sophie.

So I shook my head again. "They were just sentences," I said. "They weren't real."

"Oh." Mrs. Kwon nodded. "I see. Okay, well, in that case, great job."

"So can I go?"

"Yes, you may." She stood up, and so did I. We walked to the doorway. I wasn't sure if I was still going to get my hug. Maybe teachers weren't allowed to hug you if the rest of the class had already left. There was probably a rule against that. So I just waved goodbye and left the classroom.

I'd taken a few steps down the hall when Mrs. Kwon called after me, "Cassidy, hold on."

I stopped and turned around.

She walked up and put her hand on my shoulder. When she leaned down, I got the faintest whiff of her strawberry shampoo. "I know they were just made-up sentences, but even in a made-up world, it's not such a good idea to try to coax someone to like you. It usually doesn't work. And the truth is,

94

the best kinds of friends don't need to be coaxed. They like you just the way you are."

This sounded right. But it also sounded wrong. I was already being myself, and Lucy London didn't like me.

"Okay," I said. Because what else was I supposed to say?

Mrs. Kwon smiled and patted my shoulder.

Chapter Sixteen

Dad and Sophie were in the kitchen at the stove when I got home. The birdhouse was still sitting in the middle of the kitchen table.

"Guess what, Cass?" Sophie said. "Dad and I solved the egg problem!"

"You did?"

"Yep. Hard-boiled! No egg cracking necessary. Now I'm going to be self-reliant in the mornings just like you, and I can eat eggs whenever I want to make them."

"That's a great solution."

Sophie grinned. "I thought of it myself. Well, with help from Mom and Dad and Debra. At first, Mom was like, you can be self-reliant by pouring a bowl of cereal or making toast or something. And I was like, but I love eggs. And Dad was like, what if Mom cracked the eggs for you and you could learn how to fry them up? And I was like, but I want to be able to do it all myself. And then Debra was like, maybe you can make a sticker chart to help you deal with your fear about the egg goo getting on you, and I was like, I think I'm too old for sticker charts. But then I did end up making a sticker chart, and the first sticker I earned was for holding an egg for a whole minute in my bare hands, and I did it yesterday with Dad, and while I was holding it I was thinking I would be way less scared if the egg were cooked and couldn't maybe break and get all over me. And then I was like, ta da, that's it! Hard-boiled eggs! You know, Cass, fried eggs aren't all they're *cracked* up to be." Sophie laughed. "Get it?"

I got it. "Good one."

"You okay?" Dad asked me.

I nodded.

I wished I could think of a solution for my problem that was as simple as hard-boiled eggs.

I picked up the birdhouse. "Can we hang this now, Dad?"

"Oh, honey, we have to have a snack, then get to OT and your voice lesson. And tonight's Sophie's assembly, so dinner will be early. How about tomorrow?"

"Clementine almost killed Shel Silverstein this morning, Dad!"

"Mom told me. How about I call the Bergers and ask them to keep Clementine inside?"

"You'll call now?"

"Yes. Right away."

"And we'll put up the birdhouse tomorrow?"

"You have my word." Dad hugged me. "You're a caring girl, Cassidy Sunshine."

※

At the voice studio, Javier ran his hands through his hair. "Are you all right, my friend?"

My voice had been all squeaky during warm-ups and the first verse of "Summer Sky." It wasn't easy to sing when you had friendship troubles. I considered explaining that to Javier, but I decided instead to tuck my feelings into my junk drawer and concentrate.

"Yep," I said, eyes on my music. "I'm fine."

"Okay, then let's try it again. But first, tell me what you think the lyrics mean. Is she only talking about a tree house here or is it something more than that? Something deeper?"

The chorus of "Summer Sky" went: *The tree house made of dreams and schemes illuminated by sunbeams, forgotten rotten to the core in pieces on the forest floor.*

I said, "It's about how you have to appreciate things while you have them, because they could disappear."

"Exactly. So when you're singing, you need to be communicating that idea, right?"

"Right."

He smiled at me. "Okay, great, here we go then. From the top."

He strummed the opening chord on his guitar, and I sang, but I guess I didn't really want to think about good things going away. Like friends, for instance.

Afterwards, Javier looked through some of his song files. He said, "Let's see if we can find a new piece to work on."

"Yeah, maybe something happier," I said. "'Summer Sky' is kind of a trickster song. The melody's happy, but once you listen carefully to the lyrics, it's like oh, wow, that stinks."

Javier squinted at me like he was considering my words seriously. Then he nodded and went back to flipping pages.

I studied the practice room walls. It seemed like every week I spotted an album cover I hadn't noticed before.

One cover near the ceiling had a bright orange sun with yellow rays coming out of it. "What's that one?" I asked Javier, pointing.

He looked up. "Veronica Rashid. *The Golden Drum*."

"Is it happy?"

Javier laughed. "Sort of. Kind of. Maybe not really." He scratched his head. "Actually, I'll leave that up to you, my friend. That's the thing about music." He found the title song from the album in his file and handed it to me. "You're sure you're okay, Cassidy?"

I nodded and studied the lyrics. The song seemed to be about keeping things light and breezy.

Perfect.

§

Dad downloaded the Veronica Rashid song for me after we got home from voice. I went up to my room, turned off the light, closed my blinds, and lay on my bed. Then I listened to the song on repeat. The music surrounded me, seeping into my body. I liked that feeling, being immersed in a song. But the more I listened to the words, the more I wondered if maybe it was tricking me. Happy on the surface but sad underneath, just like "Summer Sky." What if that was the truth for every song?

I turned it off. I really missed Dani. It wasn't as if we spent every minute together before, but I always knew she was there.

I opened the blinds and the window. The leaves on the tree were half gone. Soon I'd have to deal with skeleton tree, but for now, Eli Fleishman and his bedroom were safely hidden behind golden leaves. Shel Silverstein wasn't there, so I called his name and waited.

After a minute, he appeared, floating to a perfect landing on the branch outside my window.

"How was your day?" I asked.

He shuddered.

"Yeah, mine too. Poop-emoji times a hundred. Lucy hated my idea to put on a musical. And I have no idea how to fix things with Dani. She's not mean to me, like Lucy London. But she doesn't stick up for me, either. Don't I deserve a friend who sticks up for me?"

Shel Silverstein chirped.

I chirped back.

I started to feel a little better. So I sang him a song from my musical. I think he liked it. I know I did because I started to get that bubbly feeling inside.

Mom knocked on my door and poked her head in. "Hi, Sunshine, whatcha doing?"

"Just singing with Shel Silverstein."

She laughed. "He really is a special bird, isn't he?"

"I know it sounds silly, but sometimes I think he's a human trapped inside a robin's body."

Mom raised her eyebrow.

"I mean, not really," I said. "But there is something magical about him. Don't you think?"

"I don't know. Maybe. I know there's something magical about *you*." She ruffled my hair.

"Mom, I'm serious. He is not a normal bird. He cares about me. And Sophie too. The other day when Sophie and I were raking the leaves, it was almost like he was hanging out with us. And I understand his thoughts. We talk to each other. Well, not talk. But communicate."

Mom laughed. "I get it, my goofy girl. I'm glad you have each other. But I have a very important question for you."

"Yeah?"

"Is your homework all done?"

That wasn't an important question at all. "Um, I only have one math worksheet, but can I do it later?" The one thing I knew about long division was that you should put it off for as long as possible.

"I suppose you can do it after the assembly. But do me a favor, sweetie. I need ten minutes to take a quick shower. Dinner's going to be rushed tonight. Can you go over Sophie's part for the assembly with her? Help her practice it so she's confident when she goes up on stage."

"Okay."

"Great!" She kissed me on the forehead. She smelled like coffee and flowers.

I went to Sophie's bedroom. Her walls were light green, like mint chip ice cream. And all her bedding was lavender. It was a good combination. There were piles of cut-up clothes all over the floor. She must have been designing again. Scissors were hard for Sophie, but once she decided she wanted to be a fashion designer, she got motivated to master them, no matter how challenging it was. Sometimes Sophie's designs malfunctioned, like when she attempted to make socks with fringe around the top, but she cut off the toes instead. Mom was not cool with having to buy so many new socks.

Sophie was rearranging her rock collection on a window ledge when I walked into her room. Her favorite rock was an amethyst, which was a cool purple crystal. I liked the white quartz best. It was pointy at the top but not sharp.

"Look, Cass," she said. "I'm putting our favorites right next to each other. Then I'm arranging the rest by size and also by color. Do you want to hold yours for a while?"

She gave me the crystal. It fit perfectly in my hand.

"But it's not really yours," Sophie said. "I'm just letting you hold it."

"I know." I looked out Sophie's window. The sun was setting, and the sky was striped pink and purple. It was like a painting. Eli Fleishman once told me the sky turned colors at sunset because of air pollution.

Then again, Eli Fleishman didn't know anything.

"Hey, do you want me to help you with your part for tonight?" I asked.

Sophie shook her head. "It won't be hard. It's just reading from a book."

"Well, Mom wants you to practice."

"You know what would be better?" Sophie said.

"What?"

"Making wishes on our favorite crystals."

I loved making wishes. "Okay."

"You have to close your eyes," Sophie said. "And don't tell me your wish. Or it won't come true."

I closed my eyes and felt the quartz, heavy and solid in my hand. I pressed the pointy part with my thumb and thought about wishing for Lucy to like me. But that was a selfish wish. Selfish wishes never came true.

So I wished that Sophie would shine at the assembly. I had a feeling she might be wishing the same thing, and I hoped that our two wishes, on two crystals, would be extra powerful.

I opened my eyes.

"Did you finish?" Sophie asked.

"Yep."

"Me too."

Chapter Seventeen

Dad called, "Soup's on!"

He said that every night, even though we almost never had soup.

Sophie had finished arranging her rocks, so it was no problem for her to head downstairs. We needed to set the table.

Sophie took out placemats while I got the plates. "What's for dinner, Dad?" she asked.

"Spaghetti with meat sauce."

"Yum!" Sophie pumped her fist in the air.

Pasta was on my won't-ever-eat list. I choked on a noodle when I was little, and I hadn't touched the stuff since. But I smelled garlic bread baking, so no problem. I would spread the meat sauce on the garlic bread and eat it like a sandwich. "Italian style Sloppy Joes for me."

"You sure you don't want to try the spaghetti?" Dad said. "You were three when you choked on that noodle. I think you've learned how to chew and swallow since then."

"No, thank you." I followed Sophie into the dining room with the plates.

Sophie turned around and made a monster face. "Attack of the killer noodles!" She chased me around the dining room table.

I squealed and ran.

Then Mom appeared and said, "Girls! Settle down. Cass, you're going to drop those plates."

"No, I won't." I put the plates down one at a time in front of each of our seats. "See?" I twirled and curtsied.

"Amazing," Mom said. "Goofball." She looked at her watch. "But let's finish setting the table or we're going to be late."

I did the napkins and silverware. Sophie was supposed to do the glasses and water pitcher, but it wasn't easy for her to settle down. She kept laughing in that barky way and saying she was a noodle monster. A little laughter for Sophie was okay, but too much could be a problem.

"Sophie," Dad said in a warning voice.

"I'm okay-I'm okay-I'm okay," she said.

"Take a deep breath," Mom said.

Sophie took a deep breath. Then another. Then she finished setting the table.

I put the birdhouse in the middle of the table, as a centerpiece, and reminded Dad of his promise to hang it tomorrow after school.

We all sat down and helped ourselves to the food. Mom complained to Dad about the budget thing she had to do, and Dad complained to Mom about an order that got messed up for a big client. Then Mom said, "Enough! Tonight's Sophie's night. Are you excited, honey?"

"Yes," Sophie said, but she pushed her food around on her plate and made a face. "There are mushrooms in the sauce."

"You love mushrooms," Dad said.

"Not anymore," Sophie said. "They're slimy."

"You can pick them out," Mom said.

"But they're touching everything else. Their slime is everywhere."

Mom gave Dad a look, as if he should have known Sophie would suddenly decide mushrooms were slimy.

I ate my meat sauce sandwich.

"Soph, do you want some garlic bread? Or salad?" Dad said.

"I'm not hungry."

Uh-oh.

"Sophie, you've got to eat something," Mom said.

"Fine. I'll have salad." She ate one piece of lettuce. Then she pushed her food around her plate some more.

Mom said, "Soph, can you take three more bites?"

Sophie looked at her food as if it were a plate of worms. "I don't think so."

"Maybe she's nervous," I said. "I was nervous before my assembly. Remember? Are you nervous, Soph?"

"Maybe, I guess," she said.

Mom's nostrils flared. "Well, not eating is not going to help," she said in her natural consequences voice. "And now we're running late. You're making a choice, Sophie Ann, not to eat. And you realize that's not a great choice, but it's your choice."

"I'm fine, Mom!"

Mom brought some of the dishes from the dining room into the kitchen. Her heels clicked on the wood floor.

Dad said, "Sophie, how about you go to the bathroom?"

"I don't have to go," she said.

Oh no. She was doubling down. Sophie's sensory issues weren't only about how things felt on the outside. A lot of time, it was about her insides too. Like being hungry, or having to go to the bathroom, or having a muscle cramp, or feeling sad or mad or antsy. All those things could overload Sophie's senses and then she might get dysregulated.

"Sophie," Dad warned. Then he took a deep breath. "I'll give you a handful of M&M's if you go to the bathroom right now."

Mom hated when Dad bribed Sophie like that, but Mom was in the kitchen, so she didn't know. Sophie went for it. She left for the bathroom.

"Can I have M&M's for going to the bathroom?" I asked.

Dad laughed. "Fine."

❧

We headed out for the assembly at the same time Eli Fleishman and his family were coming out of their house. I wished we could just wave hello and keep walking, but Mom and Dad started talking to Eli's parents as if they were best friends reunited after summer vacation. The sky was turning dark blue, and it was cold enough to button my jean jacket.

I stopped to tie my shoe, hoping Eli would walk ahead. But when I stood up again, he was right there, waiting for me. Eli had way more freckles on the left side of his face than on the right. It was distracting. Especially when he was so close to me.

I took a step back.

He said, "Isn't it funny how we live right next to each other and our families are like the same but opposites?"

We started walking together. I asked, "Like how?"

"Like you have two girls in fifth and sixth grade, and we have two boys in fifth and sixth grade. And your dad works from home, and my mom works from home. And your sister has a disability, and I have a disability."

I tripped on a crack in the sidewalk and almost fell. Eli Fleishman had a disability?

He'd said it like it was so obvious, but it wasn't to me. I had no idea. I didn't want to make a big deal out of it, though, and I didn't want to ask him what kind of disability he had. I hated when people asked me all kinds of questions like that about Sophie. So I just said, "Yeah, that is kind of funny."

Who would have thought that Eli Fleishman and I had so much in common? If I'd wanted to be his friend, it would have been easy. But he was my secret mortal enemy. What he'd said reminded me, though, that Lucy London had a sister in sixth grade. So this was another thing we had in common. Lucy's sister, Grace, was in Sophie's actual class. I wondered if Lucy and Grace were good friends. Sometimes Sophie and I were, but sometimes we weren't. I wondered if Lucy liked being the younger sister. Sometimes I liked it, but most of the time I felt like I was actually the older sister. These were all things I could talk to Lucy about. Things that would make us better friends.

We were almost at the school when I had an amazing idea.

106

I left Eli behind and ran to catch up to my family. I slipped my hand in Mom's. "Can we go out for ice cream after? To celebrate?" I kept my voice low so that Eli's parents wouldn't hear me.

Mom said, "That sounds like fun."

"And can we invite Lucy London and her family to go with us? Her sister's in Sophie's class."

"I don't see why not."

"Hooray!" I squeezed Mom's hand to say thanks, then walked with Sophie the rest of the way.

❧

Inside the school, the halls were crowded with parents and families. Alien invaders. The sixth graders' art was displayed up and down the main hall, on tables, and hanging on the walls.

Sophie said, "You have to see my sculpture!" She pushed through the crowds, looking for her masterpiece.

We followed behind, Mom apologizing to anyone Sophie bumped into along the way. I watched for Lucy so I could invite her to join us after for ice cream. If we could hang out tonight, without all the other girls in our class, we'd have time to get to know each other better. Ice cream was pretty much scientifically proven to help you make friends. It was weird how sometimes you could think there was no solution to a problem, but if you wait a bit, the perfect solution presents itself.

"Look!" Sophie pointed to a greenish-blue ceramic blob.

"Wow!" Mom said.

"Cool!" Dad said.

"What is it?" I asked.

"It's an octopus. Duh!" Sophie laughed. "I spent a whole month making it."

I was glad she was in a great mood, despite not eating any dinner.

"Oh yeah." I turned my head to the side. "I see it now. Good job, Soph."

I thought about how Sophie wanted to be a fashion designer, but things like art and scissors were hard for her. It was pretty cool that she didn't let that stop her. She just worked harder. I wondered if I would work that hard at music if I couldn't sing on key.

Principal Walker's voice came over the PA system. "Sixth graders and families, please make your way into the gym for tonight's program. Thank you!"

"You're going to record me, right?" Sophie said to Dad. "Just like you did for Cass?"

"Yep," Dad said. "You'll be a star."

"Well, Cass is the real star. She sang. I'm just reading."

"You're still a star," Dad said.

Sophie beamed, then ran off to find her classmates.

"Good luck!" we called after her.

&

The gym was decorated like a pirate ship. All the sixth graders stood on risers on the stage. They wore bandanas or pirate hats. Sophie was in the front row. She had a red bandana wrapped around her head. It pushed her bangs down a little too much so that they were in her eyes. She also wore two strands of gold beads around her neck. I thought she looked pretty cool.

I sat between Mom and Dad in the audience. I spotted Lucy sitting one row behind me and ten seats down. I waved to her and she waved back. She was there with her mom. I didn't see anyone else with them, and I wondered if that was Lucy's whole family. I didn't know that much about Lucy London. After ice cream tonight, though, that would change.

The sixth graders sang a song about sailing and another one about a pirate mouse. I'd heard Sophie sing those songs at home.

Then Mrs. Diamond said, "Will my readers please come down?"

Sophie stepped forward with five other sixth graders, including Grace London. I elbowed Dad, and he took his phone out of his pocket and started recording. The kids shuffled around until they were in order. When Sophie seemed confused, Grace nudged her into place. They stood right next to each other.

Mom whispered to me, "You helped her prepare tonight, right, Cass?"

I thought about wishing on the crystals. That was definitely not the kind of preparation Mom meant. I shook my head. "Sophie said she didn't need to."

Mom raised her eyebrows, and I could tell she was disappointed. That's when I realized I might have messed up. Most sixth graders wouldn't need to practice reading a few lines for an assembly. But Sophie was definitely not most sixth graders.

Chapter Eighteen

Mrs. Diamond handed a book and a microphone to the first kid in line. The microphone did that high-pitched feedback thing everyone hated. I covered my ears. Sophie flinched.

Mrs. Diamond said, "Sorry about that." She motioned to the AV guy in the back of the auditorium, who turned some knobs on a big control board. Mrs. Diamond turned the mic off and on and tapped it a few times. It didn't screech. "Okay, let's try that again," she said, and handed the mic back to the first kid.

He started to read. Sophie was touching her ears, plugging and unplugging them. That loud noise must have really bothered her. I hoped she would be able to focus. Between not practicing, not eating, the microphone feedback, and the fact that she didn't seem to be paying attention to the story, Sophie was not in the best shape. I had a bad feeling in the pit of my stomach.

Sophie stopped touching her ears, but she still wasn't listening to the story. She searched the crowd for us. I waved to her, and she waved back.

The boy next to her handed her the book and the microphone. It was Sophie's turn to read. But she didn't know which line they were on. She stood there, just looking at the book.

It was quiet in the gym. Everyone was waiting for Sophie to start. But she didn't.

She didn't start.

And she didn't start.

And she didn't start.

My heart pounded. *Read!* I thought, sending her my best and strongest sister-to-sister mental telepathy instructions.

The boy next to her pointed to a line in the book, and finally

Sophie started reading. "There…was…plenty…to do…on… board."

Now my heart raced. Because not only was Sophie reading slower than a kindergartner, she was reading the part the boy before her had just read. I glanced over at Mom. Her mouth was a thin, straight line, and all the happy had left her eyes. Meanwhile, Dad was still filming Sophie on his phone.

Grace London leaned over to Sophie and jabbed her finger in the book at a different spot.

Sophie stopped and started again.

Time seemed to slow way, way down.

"Braid…Beard…glopped, no, galloped, no…"

Then she stopped. She just stood there, staring at the book.

Sophie breathed into the microphone. In and out. In and out. The sound of her breathing was way too loud.

Everyone in the gym sat there quietly, waiting. Like time had frozen and wouldn't start again until Sophie read her lines. If Sophie had a burrow, she would've climbed right in. I'd climb in with her. I felt like it was me up there on the stage. Like I was inside Sophie's body.

I grabbed Mom's arm and squeezed, but she didn't give me a reassuring look. She just stared straight ahead at Sophie. Dad slid his phone back into his pocket, a sign that, yes, this was as bad as I thought.

Everyone watched my sister. I heard a little voice from somewhere in the audience ask, "What's wrong with her? Why can't she read?" followed quickly by, "Shush, honey, that's not nice."

Sophie *could* read. It wasn't that, it was SPD. Her thermometer was breaking again.

The awkward silence in the audience changed to an awkward murmur as people started whispering and fidgeting. And then it felt like everyone was staring at us. I could almost see Mom and Dad's stress bouncing off them like sparks while everyone looked at us. Probably they were thinking, *The poor Carlson family.*

I couldn't help it, I got mad. I was especially mad that Lucy was there, witnessing it all. Not just mad. Embarrassed.

Time stood still, as if the moment was never, ever going to end.

Finally, Sophie's teacher walked out to center stage. Miss Smith stood next to Sophie and whispered something in her ear. Then Miss Smith held the microphone, so Sophie was able to point to each word as she read.

Yes! Perfect!

It wasn't that Sophie couldn't read, it was that she had trouble following the lines on the page. She almost always followed along with her finger. Or sometimes she used a special plastic reading ruler to help her eyes go where they were supposed to go.

With Miss Smith holding the microphone, Sophie was able to read like any other sixth grader. Well, kind of. She wasn't reading with any expression or emotion. Her tone was flat. They were just words on a page with no meaning.

Poor Soph. Her chance to shine was turning out horribly. It was the opposite of shining. It was one hundred percent embarrassing.

I wanted to run up on stage and give her a big hug. Tell her it was all okay. That nobody cared. But was that even true? People probably did care. I couldn't shake the feeling that everyone in the gym thought there was something wrong— something bad—about my sister.

I wondered what Lucy was thinking. I couldn't even look in her direction. I kept my eyes on Sophie.

Finally, the pirate story ended and Sophie and the other readers returned to their spots on the risers. Mrs. Diamond played the piano, and all the kids sang another song about sailing. I recognized this one. It was Sophie's favorite. But

Sophie wasn't singing. She stood there frowning. It looked like she was trying not to cry.

She was embarrassing herself even more now. Everyone was probably still looking at her. Couldn't she just sing the song? Couldn't she fake a smile?

I wanted to rescue my sister, but there was nothing for me to do.

And just when I thought it couldn't possibly get any worse, Sophie walked off the stage in the middle of the song.

Mom flinched, like maybe she was going to grab Sophie, wrap her in her arms and take her home. But Sophie had found Miss Smith, and her teacher did the job, wrapping my sister in her arms. Miss Smith whispered something in Sophie's ear. Sophie nodded, and I watched her take a deep breath. Her shoulders rose and fell.

Then she walked back on the stage and started to sing with her classmates. She even smiled.

I couldn't believe my sister was holding it together. It was a Super Sophie Sensation.

I was so proud of her.

❧

At the end of the assembly, Principal Walker thanked everyone for coming and reminded the sixth graders to take their art projects home. We picked up Sophie's octopus, and Dad put it in a brown paper bag that the art teacher handed us.

As we walked down the main hall, I spotted Lucy, so I went over to invite her to come out for ice cream with us.

She said, "Hey, Cass. Boring assembly, huh?"

Boring was not the word I'd use to describe it. But I shrugged. "It was okay."

"Your sister really messed up, though."

She stared at me. Then she laughed.

She laughed at my sister.

Here's what I wanted to say: "Sophie has a disability. She did the best she could."

Here's what actually came out of my mouth: "Yeah, she really did." And then I laughed too.

I laughed.

At my sister.

Suddenly I felt shaky. A lump formed in my throat, making it hard to swallow. I didn't want to be anywhere near Lucy London.

I didn't invite her to join us for ice cream. I didn't say goodbye. I just ran to catch up to my family.

I found them outside the main entrance. I slammed into Dad and wrapped my arms around his waist. I must have surprised him, because he stumbled and dropped the bag with Sophie's octopus.

Craaaaack!

Mom, Dad, and I stood there, staring at the bag on the ground.

Sophie looked horrified. She peeked inside the bag.

Her face turned red. "It broke! It broke into a million pieces!" Tears streamed down her cheeks. "Noooooo!" she shrieked.

She fell to the ground and started a Super Sophie Tantrum right in front of school. All the kids, all the parents, all the grandparents...everyone watched my sister wail and flail and scream her head off.

Mrs. Walker came over. A few teachers walked up too. Mom and Dad and I stood there, frozen.

Then a miracle occurred. Shel Silverstein appeared, and he circled overhead. What in the world was he doing here at night? It was way too dark for him to be out. But here he was, clearly worried about Sophie.

Mom bent down and tried to pat Sophie's shoulder, but Sophie's arms were swinging. It was always risky to get too close to Sophie when she was out of control.

"It's okay. We can glue it," Mom said.

Dad said, "Shh, Soph, shhh."

I couldn't say anything at all. I looked up at Shel Silverstein and felt a glimmer of comfort.

Sophie kept wailing.

This was all my fault. If I hadn't laughed at Sophie with Lucy London, I wouldn't have crashed into Dad, and he wouldn't have dropped the bag. I wished I could go back in time and change what I did. Or flash forward in time to when I would be alone in my room, away from the school assembly. Away from all these people. Away from Sophie's public tantrum. Away. Away. Away.

That's when I saw Lucy and Grace, standing a few feet from me, watching Sophie's meltdown. Both were smiling. They looked happy, as if the scene was entertaining for them.

Humiliation and anger swirled around inside me. I caught Lucy's eye and glared at her. She kept that amused smile on her face.

Then their mom stepped in. Sharon rushed them past us, as if we were a car wreck, too horrible to look at.

Chapter Nineteen

Sophie kept crying. She wept and wailed the entire way back to our house. I felt like crying, too, but didn't.

It took a long time to get her home. When the Fleishmans passed by us, Eli's mother smiled gently at Mom. Eli waved at me, but I pretended not to see.

I was sad for my sister, but even sadder for myself. And embarrassed. And angry. If only I had a regular family without SPD. If only I didn't have to worry about Sophie and her emotions. If only Lucy London hadn't moved to town. If only my friendship with Dani wasn't over for good. I couldn't be best friends with her anymore because there was no way I would ever be friends with Lucy London.

If only I hadn't laughed at my sister.

My legs felt heavier and heavier as we got closer to home.

Shel Silverstein was following us, landing on bushes and fence posts, flying back and hopping along the sidewalk behind us. He kept chirping in a way that seemed to say, *Poor Sophie! Is she okay? Are you okay?*

I wanted to tell him no, Sophie wasn't okay and I wasn't okay, and nothing would ever be okay again.

Suddenly, the air changed.

I turned around in time to see a blur of fur.

Clementine pouncing.

Feathers flying.

Shel Silverstein in Clementine's mouth!

"No!" I lunged. Grabbed. Got a fistful of fur.

But Clementine was gone, darting between the fake tombstones in our neighbor's yard.

I ran after her until Sophie yelled, "Cass, come back, he's here! Shel Silverstein's here."

I stopped and turned around. Mom, Dad, and Sophie were squatting around something on the ground.

No. Not Shel Silverstein. That could *not* be Shel Silverstein.

I walked over and fell to my knees. Shel Silverstein was lying on his side, quiet and still. His eyes were open but he was not moving.

"Is he okay?" Sophie asked.

I didn't know. I was afraid to touch him.

"Mom?" I asked, my voice shaking.

"Oh, Sunshine." She gently turned Shel Silverstein right side up.

I whispered, "Please, Shel Silverstein, wake up."

I held my breath.

"Please," I repeated. "Your family will be looking for you in the spring. You have to wake up!"

Dad rubbed my shoulder.

I stared at Shel Silverstein, willing him to breathe.

And then, he shuddered. He got to his feet. He shook his head.

"Shel Silverstein!"

He looked at me, but something was different. His beady black eyes were just regular bird eyes. He still had the missing piece, but the knowing stare was gone. It was him, but it wasn't. He no longer looked at me like he knew me.

"Shel Silverstein?" I asked, as if to say, *Is that you?*

He chirped. It sounded like a regular robin chirping. He wasn't trying to tell me anything. He was just making bird noises.

Another chirp.

He flew up, up, up and away, disappearing into the night.

My stomach sank. My heart crumpled like paper.

"Thank goodness he's okay!" Mom said.

Sophie said, "He came back to life!"

Dad said, "He wasn't dead, honey. He was just stunned. Good thing Clementine dropped him." Dad kissed my forehead. "I left a message for the Bergers today, honey. They must not have gotten it. I'm so sorry."

I couldn't speak.

"Look!" Sophie said. "He left a feather behind." She picked it up and handed it to me.

❧

We went inside our house, and Dad put the bag with Sophie's broken sculpture in the laundry room. Mom told her again that they could glue it back together later and everything would be fine.

"Glue it right now!" Sophie demanded, spit flying out of her mouth.

Mom took a deep breath, clearly on her last nerve. "Sophie," she said. "It's too late to start a project like that tonight."

I ran my fingers over Shel Silverstein's feather. It was silky and smooth. I couldn't believe he was gone. That connection we had...gone. Just like my connection with Dani.

Dad said, "How about we all have ice cream sundaes? We don't have to go out. We can make them right here."

Sophie asked, "Do we have sprinkles?"

Dad opened the cabinet to check. "We do."

"Okay," Sophie said, her mood lifting.

My stomach was in knots, but I told myself to hold it together. Sophie was still dysregulated, and I didn't want to set her off. "Do we have whipped cream?" I asked.

Mom opened the fridge to check. She moved things around to see if there was a can of whipped cream hiding in the back. "Oh, sorry, honey. No whipped cream."

That shouldn't have been a big deal. Of course not. So then why did I feel tears well in my eyes?

"You okay?" Mom said. "Your bird's all right. Just a little shaken up, but he's a survivor."

"I know. I'm fine." I forced a Cassidy Sunshine smile.

"Good," Mom said.

Mom pulled vanilla ice cream out of the freezer and chocolate and caramel sauce from the fridge. Dad got bowls and spoons and sprinkles. Mom scooped ice cream into the four bowls.

"That was a pretty crazy night," Sophie said, standing at the counter and squeezing chocolate sauce onto her ice cream.

I put caramel on mine.

"It sure was." Mom handed Sophie the jar of sprinkles. "I'm curious, Soph. What did Miss Smith say to you when you walked off the stage?"

Sophie shook the rainbow sprinkles all over her sundae. "She told me it wasn't my fault. That she should have thought about how it would be hard for me to hold the microphone and the book at the same time. And also that I was her best singer so she needed me to start singing. So that's what I did."

I didn't put any sprinkles on my sundae. What good were sprinkles without whipped cream?

We carried our ice cream over to the kitchen table and sat down. I tucked Shel Silverstein's feather inside his birdhouse.

"That's a good idea, Cass," Sophie said. "Now he'll know it's his home."

But I wasn't sure Shel Silverstein would even know his way to our yard anymore.

"You know what, Soph?" Mom said. "I'm really proud of you. You were feeling uncomfortable, and you asked for help. And then you listened and took that helpful advice. That was brave of you."

"Thanks, Mom," Sophie said.

"An ice cream toast to Sophie," Dad said, and held his spoon out.

I took a huge spoonful of ice cream with caramel sauce and held it out. Then we all clinked our spoons together.

I swallowed the sweet cold ice cream, with the even sweeter caramel sauce. Had Sophie really been brave to ask for help? Wouldn't the brave thing have been to sing without asking for help? I thought being brave was dealing with things on your own.

But that had not been working out well for me lately. I licked my sticky lips. I couldn't figure out how to save my friendship with Dani. I couldn't protect Shel Silverstein from Clementine. I couldn't keep Sophie from having a Super Sophie Tantrum in public. And I couldn't even stop myself from laughing at my own sister.

Suddenly I had brain freeze. I stirred my melting sundae, not wanting to eat another spoonful. I tried to shove the sad feelings into my junk drawer, but there didn't seem to be any room left. That drawer was stuffed full to overflowing.

"You okay?" Mom asked me again.

I was going to nod, not because I was okay, but because that's what I did when someone asked me if I was okay. But what if Sophie knew something I didn't? What if, in this case, she really was the big sister? The older and wiser sister. What if walking off the stage and asking for help while everyone watched was the bravest thing she could have done?

I looked at Mom and shook my head. "No, and I think I need your help."

Chapter Twenty

Mom and I sat on my bed. I wrapped myself up in my blanket. We were cozy and it felt safe enough that I could tell her what was going on.

I said, "None of my friends like me anymore."

Saying those words out loud was hard. It made the situation feel very real.

Mom's eyes got sad. "What do you mean?"

I told her everything. How nobody had stopped to help me when I fell at recess. How Lucy London made fun of me when I tried to do hip-hop, and how she wouldn't let me be in their dance club. How she told everyone my idea to put on a musical was dumb. Even how Shel Silverstein didn't seem like Shel Silverstein anymore.

I didn't tell Mom that I'd laughed with Lucy about Sophie. I couldn't admit that to her, or to anyone.

Mom hugged me and rubbed my back. That was when all the tears I'd been fighting for days finally spilled out.

Mom said, "Cassidy, love, I'm so sorry you have to deal with this. But it sounds like the problem is Lucy, not all of your friends."

"But Lucy London's the leader."

"That may be, but that doesn't mean she's in charge of everyone else."

"You don't understand," I said. "She is. It's the Lucy-factor. Nobody likes me because Lucy doesn't like me, and I don't even know why. Even Dani, Mom."

"Dani? Really?"

I nodded. "Especially Dani." I thought about how Dani went along with everything Lucy said and did. How she made me feel like I was an old worn T-shirt while Lucy was the latest style.

"Oh, honey. Lucy is the new girl, and that makes her interesting and sort of sparkly, so maybe Dani is enjoying getting to know her. But Dani loves you."

I wished I could be so sure. "I just need Lucy to like me. Then everything will be okay."

"Let me ask you something, Cass. Do you like Lucy?"

Did I? Lucy London was smart. And she had fun recess ideas. She was pretty and cool and she laughed a lot. But sometimes she laughed at people, not with people. I didn't like that. And I didn't like how she made me feel excluded. And I for sure didn't like the way she looked down on Sophie.

"I guess I don't like her as much as I used to," I said. "But I still want her to like me because I want everyone to like me."

"It's impossible for everyone to like you," Mom said. "In fact, there's only one person that you need to make sure likes you. Do you know who that is?"

"You?"

"Nope. But I do like you, by the way. And I love you." Mom kissed my nose. "The one person you need to be sure likes you is you."

"I like me," I said, and I laughed. It seemed like such a silly thing to say.

"Good," Mom said. "If you keep being your sunshiny self, and don't worry too much about Lucy London, things will settle down and work themselves out."

I thought about how I'd laughed at Sophie behind her back. I thought about how I wanted to pull Lucy's ponytail out of her head. I thought about my deep-down secret wish. "But what if I'm not sunshiny?" I whispered.

Mom whispered back, "That's okay too."

"But I'm your Cassidy Sunshine," I said.

Mom nodded. Then she did a weird smiley frowny thing,

like her mouth was smiling but her eyes got watery and sad. It made me think of the song Javier had given me. Happy and sad mixed together. Maybe it wasn't just songs that were like that. Maybe everything in life was both happy and sad.

"Remember that time we flew to Grandma and Grandpa's house in Florida?" Mom asked. "Remember how it was cloudy and gray here, and the plane flew up and through the clouds?"

"Yeah."

"What did you see once we got through the clouds?"

"A bright blue sky." I remembered the surprise and happiness I felt at the time.

"Exactly. The sun is always there, even when we can't see it. And that sunshiny quality is always inside of you, too, even when you're sad or mad or confused or whatever."

I liked thinking of my sunshine that way. "So right now I'm cloudy," I said.

"Exactly."

I liked picturing myself as a gray rain cloud. And I guess I liked being able to ask Mom for help too.

Mom yawned. "I'm beat." She got up from my bed.

"Wait, Mom. What about Shel Silverstein?"

"I don't know, honey. Some things in life defy explanation, and relationships with animals can be that way. Let's see what happens."

I didn't like waiting to see, but I supposed I had no choice. "One more thing," I asked Mom. "Does Eli Fleishman have a disability?"

"Why do you ask?"

"He said something, and it kind of surprised me."

Mom nodded and said, "Lots of people have invisible disabilities, like Sophie has. That's why it's important to treat people with kindness and respect. You never know what they might be struggling with."

"That makes sense."

Mom picked up a page of my script from the floor. "What's this?"

"Ugh. It's the musical I was writing."

"The one Lucy doesn't like?"

I nodded.

Mom read the page. "Hey, this is pretty good! Do you like the script?"

"I thought I did."

"Well then, keep working on it. You don't need Lucy's approval."

Maybe Mom was right. I liked my musical idea. And maybe if Dani had heard about the musical without Lucy around, she would have liked it too. When I first mentioned it at recess, she'd seemed into it.

I didn't want to get my hopes up. I'd already tried so many ways to fix things with Dani, and so far nothing had worked. But maybe I'd been going about it all wrong. I'd been Cassidy Sunshine, trying to make Dani happy. Trying to make everyone happy. But perhaps it was time for a change in the weather.

I hopped out of bed and gave Mom a hug.

My bedroom door opened, and Sophie came in. She was already in her pajamas. "Whatcha doing?" she asked.

"Cass is about to get ready for bed," Mom said.

"Well, I might have to work on my musical for a little while first," I said.

"What musical?" Sophie asked.

"Just something I'm writing for my friends to do at recess."

"Cool. Can I help?"

I did not want Sophie to help. It would be hard enough to get my friends to go against Lucy on this. If Sophie were involved, it would be practically impossible.

I sat on the floor and blocked Sophie's view of the script. "It's just for my friends," I said.

"But I'm your friend." She sat right next to me and peered over my hand.

"You're my sister."

"And your friend." She waved her arm in my face, showing me the friendship bracelet I'd made for her. "Right, Mom?"

I knew Mom was way past her last nerve. She would say and do anything to keep Sophie from having another temper tantrum. I didn't want Sophie to lose it either, but I needed this to be my own thing. So before Mom could tell me that I had to let Sophie help, I gathered the pages of my script into a pile and said, "You're my friend, Soph. But this is for my fifth-grade friends only."

Sophie frowned as if I'd punched her. Then her face turned red and she wailed, "That's not faaaaaiiiirrrrr!"

Not again! Sophie's voice hit me, and something snapped. All the good feelings from my talk with Mom disappeared, and the rain cloud inside me burst into a giant thunderstorm.

I yelled, "Get. Out. Of. My. Rooooooom!"

Sophie blinked. Tears filled her eyes. Mom looked shocked. Dad came running in and asked, "What's going on?"

Sophie picked up one of the pages of my script.

"Don't touch that! It's mine!" I grabbed it from her, but she didn't let go, and the page ripped in half.

My thunderstorm turned into a tornado. "Look what you did! You always ruin everything!"

Sophie was crying. Again. Dad patted her back.

"Cassidy," Mom said in a warning voice, but I was tired of always saying and doing what Sophie needed.

"No! I don't care! I wish...I wish I were an only child!"

And there it was. My deep-down secret wish, out in the open.

My heart lurched. What had I done? If I could have swallowed my words back inside, I would have. But the secret was out. It hung in the room like another dark cloud.

Here's what I thought would happen next: Sophie would

scream and cry until we were both old enough to get married and have children of our own.

Here's what actually happened: Sophie took a startled breath and stopped crying. She said, "I'm sorry, Cass. I'm sorry about your script."

Then she ran out of the room.

"Wow," Mom said, blowing out a breath. She plopped onto my bed and patted the spot next to her. I climbed up and Mom wrapped her arms around me. I was breathing hard and felt all wobbly inside.

Dad went to check on Sophie.

I waited for Mom to tell me that I'd been mean. That I needed to apologize. That I shouldn't have said something so horrible to my sister. But she didn't say anything at all. She just rubbed my back.

After a long while she pulled away and said, "Cass, honey, I know it's hard to always be a good sister to Soph, and you are. You really are. You have such a caring, kind heart and an excellent brain, and I am so sorry if I—if your dad and I—put too much pressure on you to always be your best self. And to always consider Sophie first. Because that's impossible, you know? Nobody is their best self all the time. I know I'm not. And as much as we all love Sophie, she doesn't need us to put her first all the time. That's not good for anyone. Not even Sophie. Okay?"

I nodded.

Mom held my chin and stared into my eyes. "I want you to know that no matter what, whether you're sunshiny or cloudy or something in between, I love you. You understand?"

I did. I felt empty and full at the same time. I couldn't speak. Tears leaked out of my eyes, and Mom wiped them away.

There was a knock on my door and Sophie said, "Can I come in?"

I said to Mom, "You can't make me let her help with the play."

"I won't," Mom said. "I promise. I hear you."

"Thank you," I said. Then I told Sophie she could come in. She held out a roll of tape.

"Do you want to do it or can I?" she asked.

I knew if Sophie tried to tape it, it would be messier than if I did it. But I also knew it would make her happy to put the script back together again. And I liked that she was asking me rather than making a demand. So I said, "You can tape it."

She lay on the floor and lined up the jagged edges of the page from my script. Then she ripped off a long piece of tape, her tongue sticking out in concentration. The tape stuck to her fingers and got tangled, so she needed a new piece.

I said, "It might be easier if you do a few short pieces instead of one long one."

She ripped off a short piece. But when she tried to tape the paper together, the paper moved. I could see she was getting frustrated. So I lay down next to her and held the paper while she taped it. We were practically nose to nose, and I could smell her minty toothpaste breath.

Things were hard for Sophie. So many things. But that didn't mean things weren't also going to be hard for me sometimes too. I remembered Sophie's octopus, and I felt guilty all over again for my part in that accident. I knew better than to bring that up to Sophie, but I promised myself that I would never laugh at my sister again.

I didn't feel as tornadoey anymore. But that dark cloud of my deep-down secret wish was still hanging there in my room. The weird thing was, saying it out loud made me realize it wasn't even true. The true thing was that Sophie would always be my sister, and that was sometimes good and sometimes hard, but I wouldn't want it any other way. It was like east always being east. A sister was someone you could count on.

"I'm sorry I yelled at you," I whispered. "And I don't wish I were an only child."

Sophie looked up at me and smiled. "That's okay, Cass. I know." She ripped off another short piece of tape and placed it carefully on the script. And another. And another. "Sometimes I say things I don't mean when I get mad too. You might want to try to take a deep breath and let the bad feelings pass next time though."

I laughed. "I'll try to remember that."

I realized something then. No matter how much of a helper I was with Sophie, no matter how hard Mom, Dad, Debra, Jackie, all her teachers, and I tried to help Sophie stay regulated, the one person who put in the most effort was none other than Sophie Ann Carlson.

She handed me the taped-together page. "Good as new."

"Thanks, Soph," I said.

Mom said, "Okay, you two. It's way past your bedtimes. Say goodnight."

"Goodnight, Soph."

"Goodnight, Cass."

I gave my sister a hug.

Chapter Twenty-One

The next morning I woke to a commotion outside my window that sounded like a car alarm. *Ah ah ah ah!*

I opened the blinds. A flock of blue jays was at the feeder. Shel Silverstein was gone so the jays had taken over his territory. I couldn't believe it.

The jays' calls were different from the robins' sweet chirping. And the jays were messier too. They spilled the birdseed out of the feeder and onto the grass below. The blue jays on the ground were gathering up the spillage, feasting on each tasty morsel.

I watched them for a while. One of the birds pecking in the grass wasn't a jay. I pressed my forehead against the window and looked carefully. It looked like a robin. Could it be?

Shel Silverstein!

I opened the window and called down to him.

He looked up at me and cocked his head to the side. Did he recognize me? I wasn't sure. He went right back to eating with his new flock. His new friends. He'd done it!

I wanted to watch the birds all morning, but I had to get to school early enough to hang out with Dani before Lucy's bus arrived. So I got dressed, brushed my hair, and went into Sophie's room.

She was on the floor as usual, curled up under her blanket.

"Morning, Soph," I said, opening the blinds.

Sophie pulled the blanket over her head.

"I want to walk to school with you, but only if we leave by seven thirty. Not a minute later. Okay?"

"Okay," Sophie said in a sleepy voice.

"I mean it. I'm leaving at seven thirty."

"Okay," she repeated. "I'm moving."

I went back to my room and grabbed the script. Then I went downstairs to put it in my backpack. I didn't want to just shove the pages in my pack, where they could get wrinkled or ripped again, so I opened a folder to slide the script inside.

And there was my untouched homework. Long division. A whole worksheet. Rats!

With all the chaos, I'd totally forgotten about it. I'd never skipped homework before, but there was a first time for everything.

"What's that?" Mom asked, looking over my shoulder.

"Nothing." I closed the folder quickly.

"Is that your homework? The assignment you were supposed to do last night?"

I nodded.

Mom looked at her watch. "Well, you can do it while you eat breakfast. You've got time."

Double rats.

I pulled out the worksheet and a pencil and sat down at the kitchen table.

"Waffles or eggs?" Mom asked, giving me a glass of orange juice. "I'll make your breakfast today so you can do your math."

"Waffles, please." I got to work.

Soon the kitchen smelled like cinnamon, and Mom slid the waffles in front of me. I didn't put any syrup on them so I could eat with my fingers while I kept doing my homework. I looked up at the kitchen clock. 7:10. Six problems to go. Long division took so long!

Sophie bounced into the kitchen and got a hard-boiled egg out of the fridge. "Whatcha doing, Cass?"

"Homework. Can't talk."

She peered over my shoulder. "Oh, long division? I love long division. Want me to help you?"

I didn't look up from my paper. "No, thank you."

"Because I could help you. I'm really good at it. You know what else I'm good at? Making hard-boiled eggs. That's something you don't even know how to do yet. But I could teach you if you want. It's easy. For me anyway. It might not be as easy for you."

"Sophie!" I said.

"What?"

"Remember what I said about wanting to leave at seven thirty? It's seven fifteen now."

"Oh, right. So you better hurry then. I can fill the bird feeder this morning."

Mom said, "Sophie, eat your egg and let Cass do her work. I'll make sure the bird feeder is full."

Sophie left me alone, but she made lots of yummy sounds as she ate her egg.

My handwriting got a little messy, but I zoomed through the problems and finished by 7:25. Ran upstairs. Went to the bathroom. Brushed my teeth. Ran downstairs. Put on my shoes. Slid my homework and lunch into my backpack. Grabbed my jean jacket. Waved goodbye to Dad, who was in his office on the phone. Gave Mom a kiss.

It was 7:32.

Where was Sophie?

"Sophie!" I called.

No answer.

She was probably upstairs still brushing her hair or teeth. Well, too bad for her. I was leaving. She'd had an extra two minutes, and she still wasn't ready on time.

I yelled upstairs that I was leaving, then I walked out the front door.

And there, on the driveway waiting for me, stood my sister. "You said seven thirty," she said. "You're late."

I felt my Cassidy Sunshine smile, a real one, spread across my face.

We had just started walking when Eli Fleishman rushed out his front door. He called to us, "Hey, wait up!"

We stopped and waited for him.

"Check this out." Eli threw three beanbags in the air and juggled them while singing a carnival tune. "Cool, right? I taught myself from an online video. Want me to show you how?"

"No, thank you."

Sophie and I kept walking.

"It's easy," Eli called after us. "I even taught my brother. If you change your mind, let me know! I'm a great teacher!" He kept juggling while we continued on our way.

Sophie said, "Do you think he could really teach us how to juggle?"

"I don't know. But who cares? He's Eli Fleishman, my secret mortal enemy."

"Right."

We kept walking.

"But why?" Sophie asked.

"You mean why's he my enemy?"

Sophie nodded.

That was a good question. "Um, I don't remember." And the weird thing was, I didn't.

Sophie laughed. "Because he's actually kind of nice. And interesting."

That was true. I thought about "The Funky Kittens vs. The Volcano." One of the acts could be a juggler. I stopped and turned around. "Eli?"

He caught the beanbags and looked at me. "Yeah?"

"So I'm writing a musical and I was wondering if you want to be in it. You could be a juggler."

His eyes lit up. "Cool!" He turned to Sophie. "Are you in it?"

"No." Sophie's shoulders slumped. "It's just for fifth graders."

"Too bad," Eli said. "Because Trey can juggle with me, and it's twice as cool."

Hmmm. Maybe I'd been too quick to decide the play was only for fifth graders. I didn't even know if I could get my fifth-grade friends to do it.

"Well, actually," I said, "you and Trey can both be in it. And Soph, there's a job I didn't think about before that you would be perfect for."

"Really?" She smiled from ear to ear. "I'll take it."

"You haven't even heard what it is."

"That's okay."

I laughed. "You can be in charge of the audience. You can tell everyone about the show, and make tickets, and give them away. And then you can sit front row center."

"I'd be good at that."

"I know."

When we got to school, I spotted Dani standing over by the monkey bars. I said goodbye to my sister and Eli and headed toward my friend.

Chapter Twenty-Two

"Summer Sky" was going through my head as I walked up to Dani. I hoped we weren't like the song, a broken tree house on the forest floor.

A cool breeze swept in and a bunch of leaves rustled and fell to the ground. The sky was gray and cloudy. Dani swung across the monkey bars and jumped off at the other end.

"Hi," I said.

"Hi!" She gave me a warm smile. "You're here early."

"Yep, I finally got out of the house on time."

"Sweet. Do the monkey bars with me."

We got in line. Dani updated me about Rafi and his lice and her mom going bananas because she was still picking nits out of his hair. She didn't mention hip-hop or Lucy London or dance club. It was almost like we'd gone back in time and everything was normal between us again. A small part of me wanted to go along with that, keep the peace. But that was the Cassidy Sunshine part. I had to sing something true.

I looked up at the cloudy sky for inspiration. Then I dropped my backpack on the ground, and before Dani got back on the monkey bars, I said, "Dani, I need to tell you something."

She climbed the rungs and held on to the first bar. "Yeah?"

"You've really been upsetting me lately. Every time you side with Lucy instead of me, it hurts my feelings. And it makes me think I've been replaced. Like maybe you'd rather be best friends with Lucy."

She looked down at me. "Cass! Of course you're still my best friend." She reached for the next bar. "We're best friends forever."

Those were the words I wanted to hear. That was exactly

134

the kind of reassurance I had been hoping for. But somehow it didn't work. I didn't feel reassured. I felt like maybe Dani was being Dani Sunshine. Saying whatever would make me happy, even if it wasn't true.

The rule of the monkey bars was you had to wait until the person in front of you was finished, but I didn't wait. I climbed up the rungs and followed Dani.

"What about when you agreed my musical was a dumb idea?" She swung, and I swung after her. "What about when I fell at recess and you didn't stop to help me?" Swing. "What about when you gave my friendship bracelet to Lucy?" Swing. "What about when I tried to dance, and Lucy laughed at me? You didn't say anything. You let it happen! That's not how best friends treat each other!"

I was out of breath. It was hard to swing across monkey bars and yell at your best friend at the same time.

When Dani jumped off so did I.

Her eyes were watery. She blinked away her tears.

I hadn't wanted to make her cry. "I'm sorry," I said.

"No. You're right. I shouldn't have let her laugh at you. I'm sorry, really I am. But sometimes Lucy makes it hard to do the right thing. I don't know why."

Dani was right. Lucy had a weird power. The Lucy-factor. It was real, and it was strong enough to make me laugh at my own sister.

I said, "So let's just not be friends with Lucy. Let's go back to how we used to be." I wanted that with all my heart.

Dani dug the toe of her shoe into the woodchips. "I don't know, Cass. She's in our class, and I really like the dance studio, and…I don't want to cause trouble."

I felt my nose tingle like I might cry. "So, then, what?"

"I don't know."

We stood there looking at each other.

"Tell me the truth, Dani. If you want to be best friends with

Lucy instead of me, just tell me. I'd rather know." My heart sped up and my throat clogged. I felt the way I did during a thunderstorm, in the waiting time between seeing lightning and hearing the thunder.

Dani tucked her hair behind her ears. "Remember Halloween in kindergarten?"

"Of course." Dani and I had shown up in identical witch costumes. "That's when we became best friends. Because of our costumes."

"Not because of our costumes," Dani said. "Because of what you did when Eli grabbed my hat and threw it in a puddle. At that point you were basically just the girl with the pigtails who could already read chapter books while I was still on the *Pat the Cat* books. But when you saw what Eli did, you marched right over and told him that was mean and it wasn't a good way to treat people. Then you gave me your hat to wear. You ended up walking in the costume parade without a witch's hat, and people didn't know what you were supposed to be."

I remembered that someone had asked me if I was a pirate and someone else asked me if I was a dementor. But I didn't remember Eli throwing Dani's hat in the puddle or me telling him off.

"That's when we became best friends," Dani said. "Because I knew you were the kind of person I wanted to be. Someone brave and smart and kind. And the truth is, I'm still trying to be like you."

"What are you talking about? You *are* brave and smart and kind!"

Dani shook her head. "I haven't been lately. I think I really liked all the attention Lucy gave me. And for some reason, I like Lucy, even though she can be mean. But *I* don't want to be mean. Especially not to you. And I don't want to lose you as my best friend."

The buses pulled up. Lucy would be joining us any minute. I had to think fast.

"What if we stick together?" I asked. "The two of us together are stronger than each of us alone. We could still be friends with Lucy but we won't let her control us. We can promise not to do what Lucy wants us to do until after we think about it ourselves. We can help each other."

Dani was nodding while I was talking. "That's a good idea. I like it."

I wanted to be sure. I got my script out of my backpack and handed it to Dani. "Tell me the truth. Do you think this is dumb?"

Dani started reading. I watched her face. She smiled. She nodded. She laughed. When she got to the end of what I'd written so far, she looked at me. "Do you have more?"

"Not yet, but we can work on it at recess if you want."

"I want."

My heart soared.

Lucy ran up to us, her ponytail swinging. "What's that?" she asked, looking at my script.

"It's Cass's script for the musical," Dani said.

"I thought we decided that was a dumb idea," Lucy said.

"Well, really, *you* decided it was a dumb idea," I said. "But *I* still like it." I looked at Dani.

"And so do I," she said.

Here's what I thought would happen next: Lucy would raise one eyebrow with a look of disgust and say, "Then you're as big a loser as Cass is."

Here's what actually happened: Lucy raised both her eyebrows with a look of surprise, and said, "Oh."

The first bell rang. Dani handed the script back to me.

"Let's work on it at recess," Dani said.

"Great," I said. "We can pick roles."

We had started to walk toward the door to school when Lucy said, "Wait." We turned around. "Can I be in it?"

I hesitated. I didn't want to be an excluder. But I also didn't want Lucy to take over. But just because she had been bossy before didn't mean she would always be that way. Things change. People change. Talking to Dani had already made it seem like Lucy wasn't quite so powerful. Plus, Lucy wasn't all bad. Take *The Giving Tree*. Because of Lucy, I'd been able to see that book in a whole new way. I was not going to be anybody's stump. Loving someone didn't mean you had to give your whole self away. It was better to be able to sway in the breeze and still have a strong trunk rooted to the ground.

So I said, "I'm the director. And Sophie's in charge of the audience. And Eli Fleishman's going to be in it too. If that's all okay with you, then, yes, you can be in it."

Lucy said, "Okay, but are you sure I can't be the director? Maybe a co-director with you? I'm really good at directing things."

Dani said, "No. It's Cass's play. Cass is the director."

Lucy looked from Dani to me. "Okay, fine. I guess that makes sense. But maybe I can be in charge of the dance part?"

"We'll vote on it at recess," I said.

Dani and I smiled at each other.

As Dani, Lucy, and I walked into school together, I looked up at the sky. The sun peeked out between two puffy clouds.

I squinted and waved hello.

Chapter Twenty-Three

We worked on the musical every chance we could for two weeks.

Then, on a day that fell between Halloween and too-cold-outside, I ran around the playground at recess. I shouted, "If you want to see a really cool show, come to the dome. It's about to start!"

We had decided not to make tickets. And Sophie was not in charge of the audience. Instead, she had a more important role to play. While I gathered our audience, my sister was sitting on top of the dome, dressed in a red costume she'd made herself, waiting for the play to start.

We had a big cast, so even kids who weren't in the musical were friends with someone who was. And that's probably why so many people came over to see it. There must have been over a hundred kids sitting cross-legged on the playground waiting for us to begin. Even Mrs. T., the recess monitor, stood in the back to watch the show. And Sophie's aide, Miss Michelle. And Mrs. Diamond. Mrs. Kwon. Miss Smith. Even Mrs. Walker!

I felt jittery and nervous, like I'd felt before I sang my solo at the assembly. I hoped the feeling would go away as soon as I started singing, like it had then.

As I stepped over to the dome, Shel Silverstein flew by. I hadn't seen him much since he'd joined up with the blue jays. Only in the mornings at the feeder. He sometimes went inside his birdhouse, but just as often there'd be blue jays in there instead. I no longer had the feeling we knew each other, but he still seemed to like our tree.

As he swooped down from above, I caught his eye, and this

time, I got a tinge of that magical feeling. Like maybe he was coming to say hello and good luck, as if he still knew me.

He circled around a few times before flying over to a tree at the edge of the field. As soon as he got there, a flock of birds lifted up to meet him. Blue jays. Together, they flew off, traveling away from the school. Thanks to Bakiwang Says, I could see they were headed south.

So Shel Silverstein hadn't come to say hello. He'd come to say goodbye.

My heart twisted as I watched him soar away. But he was doing what he had to do to survive. And he'd be back in the spring. I was sure of it.

I turned to the audience. "Hi, everyone," I said as loudly and clearly as I could. "Welcome to the world premiere of a new musical called *The Funky Kittens versus The Volcano*. I hope you enjoy our show!"

My heart was still pounding fast as I took my place with the kids playing townspeople.

Holly, our bird narrator, walked confidently to the front of the dome and said, "On an island in Hawaii sat a giant volcano." She pointed behind her to Sophie. "It looked calm and happy, so you'd never know that deep inside, it was really, really, really, really, really, really, really, really MAD!"

Sophie's part was next. We'd practiced so much, I knew she could do it. But still, I was worried. I didn't want her to mess up this time. For her sake, and for mine.

Sophie paused. She took a deep breath. Then she made an angry face and sang out, "I'm a grumpy volcano and you know that's right. I sit by myself all day and all night. No one visits or asks what's doing. So my hot lava's bubbling, boiling, and brewing. You better run fast, better clear that road, 'cause I'm really mad, and I'm gonna explode!" She waved her fist in the air.

Some of the kids in the audience laughed, but they were laughing with Sophie, not at her. Relief rushed through me.

Holly said, "The townspeople panicked! They scattered and fled. Until one brave girl stood up and said…"

That was my cue!

I took center stage and calmed the townspeople down by singing, "Wait! Hold on! Let's not scream and shout. The volcano's just lonely and feeling left out. If we entertain it, we'll turn things around. We'll quiet those rumblings and save our whole town!"

As soon as I began to sing, the jitters and all the nervousness instantly disappeared. Now it was all about fun.

Holly said, "The townspeople listened to the brave girl's words. She had a good point, they all concurred."

Sophie's Pokémon-trading friends took the stage. Carly was wearing a top hat and a cape. Rebecca carried three metal rings and a magic wand. They sang, "We'll be the ones to save our fine town. 'Cause we're magicians, and we're world-renowned. Our tricks will astonish, amaze, and delight. That mean old volcano won't put up a fight."

Then Carly did some tricks with the metal rings, while Rebecca waved the wand and said all sorts of magical-sounding words. To be honest, the tricks weren't so good. The audience was not impressed. I hoped they wouldn't get bored and walk away.

When Sophie shook her head and roared, everyone seemed to pay attention again.

Trey and Eli came to center stage, carrying an assortment of balls. They sang, "We'll be the ones to quiet that roar. You won't believe all we have in store. A juggling routine with every size ball. From ping-pong to bowling, we'll catch them all."

And they did! They juggled alone, then they juggled together, trading balls. I was amazed. So was the audience.

But not our volcano. Sophie let out a long, loud growl.

141

Next came the acrobats, a group of kids from fifth and sixth grade.

"Don't you worry and don't you fret. We've got this covered, and it's no sweat. We'll tumble and flip and land on our feet. That awful volcano will surely be beat."

The tumblers were great, and one of the girls did about a billion back handsprings in a row. The audience loved it, but Sophie growled and gnashed her teeth and looked mad.

All the townspeople were supposed to be acting nervous and panicky, but some of them had forgotten. They were too caught up in the fun.

Shayna, Monique, and a few other girls came to the front and sang, "Hold on, we have a different idea. A sweet lullaby will set us all free, yeah. She'll listen to us and soon fall asleep. That scary volcano won't make a peep."

They sang "Rock-a-Bye Baby," but instead of putting the volcano to sleep, they put all the townspeople to sleep. The kids around me closed their eyes and pretended to snore.

The audience cracked up.

Sophie shook the top of the dome and roared, waking the townspeople and quieting the audience.

One townsperson cried, "Your plan didn't work!"

Another said, "The town is doomed!"

A third one said, "It's gonna explode!"

A fourth yelled, "We'll all be consumed!"

Holly said, "The brave girl feared she'd led them astray. The volcano's bad mood was not going away."

Then I sang, "We can't give up. Let's take one more chance. I know! We'll ask the Funky Kittens to dance!"

The townspeople cheered.

Holly said, "They're the best dancers around. Everyone hoped they'd save their fine town."

Holly was really good at memorizing lines.

Lucy, Dani, Evie, Grace, and a bunch of other dancers ran to the front of the dome. They were dressed in black and wearing cat-ear headbands and tails. Together they rapped, "We're hip-hopping kittens, we've got such pizzazz. We kick, stomp, and twirl, we are razzmatazz. If anyone can calm this fiery beast… it's us! We're as sure as east's always east."

Lucy pressed play on her music player, but nothing happened. She pressed the button again. And again.

Where was the music? Oh no!

The Funky Kittens looked at each other.

The audience squirmed.

This was our big moment, and we were stalled!

Lucy struggled with the player, her face blushing pink. Dani and I joined her. Dani turned the player off and on. Off and on. Then I saw that the portable speaker had its own power button, and it was off! I turned it on and the music came blasting out.

"Oops!" Lucy said.

Everyone laughed. Lucy mouthed "thank you" to me.

She restarted the song at the beginning, and the Funky Kittens hip-hopped their way through a totally cool dance.

The audience cheered!

Sophie cheered!

Then Sophie sang, "You've got so much power in each stomp and kick. We have that in common, it's quite a good trick. When I get mad, I roar and I growl. But then I calm down and don't feel so foul. Now that I'm calm I need to explain. Entertainment is not what I wish to attain. The truth of the matter is I want a friend, someone on whom I can always depend."

Holly said, "The townspeople weren't so sure it was smart to befriend a volcano that might blow apart. But the brave girl courageously led the way. She said—"

My cue again.

I picked up a pipe-cleaner flower from the bunch we had made at Dani's house the week before. I held it out to Sophie.

143

"I'll be your friend, starting today." Then I threw it into the dome.

One by one, everyone in the cast picked up a flower and offered it to Sophie, tossing each one into the dome.

Holly said, "Soon the townspeople erupted with laughter..."

And together, we all said, "And everyone lived happily ever after."

Sophie jumped down from the dome and joined us in a line as all the performers held hands and bowed. With Sophie on one side of me and Dani on the other, with Lucy and Eli and so many friends, the kids I'd known before and some I was just getting to know, I felt all filled up. I was full of something good, something warm and happy and true.

I tucked that feeling into my junk drawer, just in case someday I'd want to take it out and feel it again.

Acknowledgements

Thank you to my incredible nieces, Riley Baer and Billie Baer, who inspired this story. It's my great privilege to watch you grow. Your kindness, compassion, humor, and resilience make me proud to be your aunt.

Thank you to my sister, Micky Baer, for being my best friend for life and for sharing your joys and sorrows with me. When good things happen to you, they're happening to me. When hard things happen to you, they're happening to me. I know it's the same for you too. How lucky we are to have each other!

Thank you to my brother-in-law, Jeff Baer, who didn't blink when I wrote a story inspired by his family. Thank you for trusting me to get it right.

Thank you to my extraordinary critique group: Sarah Aronson, Carolyn Crimi, Jenny Meyerhoff, and Laura Ruby. You are exquisite writers and true friends. Thank you for gently encouraging me to expand a short story about one day in my nieces' lives into this novel. Thank you for never giving up on me, even when I gave up on myself.

Thank you to Joyce Sweeney for helping me get my writer's mojo back.

Thank you to Debbie Fischer and Virginia Aronson for your friendship, critiques, and encouragement. Debbie, you are my Cuban expert. And Virginia, you are the fairy godmother of editing!

Thank you to Jaynie Royal and Pam Van Dyk for believing in this story and for bringing it to readers.

Thank you to Rachel Simon, Micky Baer, and Faith Ferber for helping me consider every angle of how to write about a character with a disability. With your input, I tried my best to be appropriate and sensitive to people with disabilities and their families. Language and understanding seem to constantly change, and I hope to constantly learn and grow, too.

Thank you to Jody Smith Block. You played a critical, heroic role at the event that inspired this book, and I'm grateful that you were there for Riley with warmth, love, and wisdom.

Thank you to Julie Learner for being there for me through all the ups and downs.

Thank you to my parents, Adrienne and Neil Aaronson for everything, always.

Thank you to my children: Jacob, Faith, and Sammy, who told me it wasn't possible to quit being a writer.

And above all, thank you to my college sweetheart, the world's best husband, the man I can't imagine my life without: Alan Ferber. Thank you for loving me as I stumble through this life, always trying to sing something true.